"You're very cute, Doc, but you're not my type."

Marc blinked and sat back. The fact that he wasn't her type was certainly no news flash, but her bluntness startled him. Clearly she was feeling no pain. How ironic that her whispered vow was painful for him. Not that he'd wanted her to chase him around the office, but the idea of, well, a little mutual chasing had crept into his thoughts. "I—uh—appreciate your frankness."

"It's like this," Mimi whispered. "I won't be here for long, and no matter what you think, I don't jump into the sack for sport."

He clenched his teeth. Yes, he had made a crack like that, hadn't he? Leaning forward, he started to speak, then saw the glimmer of tears in her eyes. That stopped him dead.

"You don't like me, Doc." It wasn't a question.

He cleared his throat. "I—of course I like you, Miss _____ _____ _____ u, he went on men_____ _____ _____ 're gone. "If it mak_____ _____ _____ type, either."

D1173054

Dear Reader,

I had so much fun with my ENCHANTED BRIDES trilogy, I decided it would be exciting to write a series about three brothers. I envisaged each brother to be tough and successful in his own right, but lonely— whether he realizes it or not. Then I decided to place these men on a mountain of emeralds located on their own private island.

The heirs to the Merit emerald dynasty, Jake, Marc and Zack are as different as brothers can be. But what they have in common is that they are all gorgeous men— each about to meet one special woman for him.

I hope you enjoy Marc's story, *Coming Home to Wed*. Once a doctor in a big city, he yearned for a simpler life. He's returned home to Merit Island to settle down and the last person he expects to be attracted to is free spirit, Mimi Baptiste.

All my best,

Renee Roszel

P.S. I love to hear from readers so do, please, write to me at P.O. Box 700154, Tulsa, Oklahoma 74107.

COMING HOME TO WED

Renee Roszel

THE MERITS OF
MARRIAGE

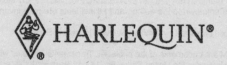

HARLEQUIN®

TORONTO • NEW YORK • LONDON
AMSTERDAM • PARIS • SYDNEY • HAMBURG
STOCKHOLM • ATHENS • TOKYO • MILAN • MADRID
PRAGUE • WARSAW • BUDAPEST • AUCKLAND

To Linda Fildew
An editor with pizzazz

ISBN 0-373-15849-1

COMING HOME TO WED

First North American Publication 2000.

Copyright © 2000 by Renee Roszel Wilson.

Visit us at www.eHarlequin.com

Printed in U.S.A.

CHAPTER ONE

THE fog that swept stealthily over the surface of the Atlantic didn't bother Marc. He liked the fog, its cloistered quiet, after long days of taking care of patients. The hours of tending to his charges were endless, but he was content. Six months after taking over old Doc Fleet's practice, he could make the crossings between Merit Island and the surrounding rocky islets with his eyes closed. Which was lucky, since his radar had gone out earlier that afternoon.

Marc inhaled the damp sea air. He smiled. The night had closed around him like a comfortable old coat, and there wasn't a sound except for the low growl from his cruiser engine as he slowly made his way home. The ocean was calm. His patients were all bandaged, medicated and reassured. Life was good, if a bit lonely.

The only trouble with being back on Merit Island was the lack of eligible women. His latest nurse, Ursula, had been attractive and enthusiastic about making their doctor-nurse relationship more than it should be. But she hadn't liked the isolation—or the fact that Marc was not as inclined toward an affair as she. So she'd quit, yesterday. Just like that. Poof! She was gone.

He was overworked and shorthanded as it was. But what country doctor wasn't? He made a small adjustment in course, sensing more than seeing his way.

That morning he'd put an ad for a nurse in several national medical publications. The salary he offered was exceptional so he knew he'd have a new assistant in a couple of weeks. Three at the most. He winced at the thought of two or three weeks without help and exhaled wearily. Meanwhile—

A jolt and a reverberating boom brought Marc out of his mental meanderings. "What the...?" Something had rammed his cruiser amidships, just behind where he sat at the helm. He flipped on the cargo lights and jumped off his seat to find out what idiot had run into him.

Moving to the side where he'd been hit, he squinted into the fog, now brightly illuminated. It wasn't hard to distinguish the front of a small catamaran, since the bows of both parallel hulls were crumpled against the side of his cruiser, exposing the smaller boat's foam-composite core. The fiberglass on the side of his cruiser was badly dented and the gelcoat finish torn up.

He bit back a curse. Out of the corner of his eye, Marc saw somebody slowly rise to stand, hooking an arm around the mast to steady herself on the canvas trampoline. Marc's frown deepened when he realized the one-man strike force was a petite blonde. What was she doing out here alone in a fog?

After a quick, horrified look at the mangled hulls of her boat, she let out a wail and fisted a hand in her unfettered mass of hair. "Oh, no!" Her gaze lifted to fix on Marc and she jabbed a finger at the damage to her prow. "Look what you did to my boat!"

Marc eyed her with annoyed disbelief. "How thoughtless of me to ram the side of my boat into the front of yours." He made the remark with distinct, sarcastic overtones. "Try to forgive me."

She ran a shaky hand through her hair, plainly agitated. "But—but this isn't even my boat!"

"I suppose you were just passing by when

you heard the crash and decided to investigate?''

Her glance shot from the damage back to his face. ''Not that I don't appreciate stinging satire!'' she shouted. ''But it's not particularly helpful at the moment.'' Making a pained face, she shook her head. ''What am I going to do? I can't sail this thing back to shore like this! It'll sink!''

''I doubt that, but you won't be able to steer it,'' Marc said. Something dark began to ooze down her forehead and he experienced a prick of concern. ''You're bleeding.'' He indicated the spot on his own forehead. ''You must have hit your head.''

''Of course, I hit my head! I was in an accident!'' She touched the trickle and grimaced at the blood on her fingers. ''This is just *perfect*!''

''I'd better take a look at it.'' He pulled some rope from a storage cabinet, deciding he had no choice but to tie the catamaran to his cruiser. He couldn't leave a bleeding, possibly concussed woman out in a fog on a damaged boat.

''Don't bother about me, mister,'' she called. ''I can take care of myself.''

After securing the rope to his cleat, he

clambered over the side onto her damaged hull.

"What are you doing?" she demanded.

"Coming to check out your head."

"I don't have a head. This is a small boat."

"Not the bathroom," he said, trying to keep his voice calm. The woman was obviously addled. "*Your* head."

"I told you, I don't need—"

"I heard," he cut in, leaping to the canvas trampoline to tie the other end of his rope to the tramp frame. After knotting the line, he faced her. "Keep still while I look at your cut."

"You're quite the masterful sea captain." She frowned at him. "Do you marry people on the high seas, too?"

Working to hold his temper, he indicated the canvas surface. "Sit down while I examine you."

"Who do you think you are, ordering me around?"

"The guy you hit." He pressed on her shoulders. "Sit."

"Okay, but only because I'm a little— tired." She did what he asked, though clearly reluctant. He had a feeling the thump she took was starting to throb.

"You meant to say dizzy, didn't you?"

"No," she said. "I meant tired. I've been wandering around—for a while. I got a little lost in the fog."

"And you could be a little unconscious in a few minutes if you've got a concussion." He knelt beside her and cleared the hair away from her injury. He took note of her hair, a golden blond. Fishing around among the roots as he was, he could tell the color was natural, the texture, thick, and soft. He mentally shook himself. *You're a doctor, man! Get on with the business of doctoring!*

"A concussion?" she said with a short, caustic laugh. "That little bump? I've had worse jolts putting on straw hats."

He couldn't help the amused twitch of his lips. He had to give the sassy miscreant credit. She had spunk.

"Once in the Australian outback, I had to splint my own broken leg—with a couple of branches and a belt. So, you see, I can take care of myself."

Her broken leg remark surprised him. She was either delirious or a pretty salty storyteller. "That's very resourceful. And how do you treat your own comas?" he asked.

"I tell you, that cut is nothing!"

"You need stitches, Miss...." He met her gaze and took singular note of her eyes. They were big and shiny and a striking silver-gray. Fortunately they showed no signs of brain trauma.

"Baptiste," she said, sounding a little less spunky. "Mimi Baptiste."

"Well, Miss Baptiste, how good are you at stitching yourself up?"

Her eyes narrowed with her wince.

"Did I hurt you?" he asked, reaching into his back pocket for his folded handkerchief.

"Only by being in my boat's way," she muttered.

He pressed the clean handkerchief against her injury. When their glances clashed again, he presented Miss Beautiful-Gray-Eyes Baptiste with his most adamant professional expression. "Hold that there while I help you to my boat."

She stared at him. "Huh?"

He shook his head at her. "You need stitches, remember? I can't do that here."

"You bet your booties you can't, fella," she retorted. "I'm not in the habit of letting complete strangers, whose only recommendation is that they skulk around in fog banks, use a needle and thread on my head!"

He grasped her upper arm and stood, hoisting her to her feet. "Can you walk?"

"I'm not walking anyplace with you!" She resisted, but not strongly enough to get free of his hold. It was obvious she wasn't as steady as she'd like to be. Not to mention that the little catamaran wasn't the most stable flooring in the world.

He tugged her along the short hull. It dipped precariously with their weight. "Let's do this quickly or we'll get a salty bath," he said. "Grab the side and I'll hoist you over."

She gave him a look that was far from co-operative. "I don't know you, buddy! If you think I'm getting into a boat with you, you're crazier than you look."

He grabbed the gunwale to steady them and faced her. "My name is Marc Merit. I live on an island, not far from here, and I'm a medical doctor." He dipped his head in a nominal and slightly mocking greeting. "How do you do? Now grab the blasted gunwale and climb into my boat before I lose my famous self-control and heave you over the side like a rock."

"I want to see some ID."

He stared at her in disbelief. "You want what?"

"ID, buster. Anybody can say he's a doctor. An ax murderer can *say* he's a doctor."

"For that matter ax murderers can *be* doctors." He pulled his wallet from his hip pocket. Flipping it open, he showed her his American Medical Association membership ID. "My ax murderer cards are still at the printer's."

She gave the ID a thorough once-over, then reached up to flip the plastic holders until she found his driver's license. For a long minute she scowled at the words *Marcus G. Merit, MD*.

"Well?" he coaxed.

She cast him a quick, sideways look, opened her mouth, then seemed to think better of arguing. "Okay, so you're a doctor," she grumbled. "But like you said, doctors can be ax murderers."

Marc flipped his wallet closed and replaced it in his pocket. "Yes, but statistically you have a better than even chance of running into a doctor who's more interested in keeping you well than in hacking you up."

"*That's* charming!" Chewing her lower lip, she considered him. Marc had a feeling she was figuring her options. "I don't like it," she mumbled, "but I guess I don't have much choice." Grasping the gunwale she flung up a leg but wasn't quite able to get her deck shoe hooked over the top. Marc grasped her waist and hoisted her far enough so she could get her leg over, then returned his grip to the gunwale to keep from toppling into the ocean.

Once on board, Mimi straightened and steadied herself, replacing the handkerchief on her wound. Before she had time to turn and glare at him, he'd boarded and taken her by the arm. "Sit down. If you're going to faint, you'll be closer to the deck."

Though he didn't look directly at her, he could sense her glower as he guided her to the seat beside his at the helm.

"You have a captivating bedside manner, doc," she muttered. "Where did you train, the Beavis and Butthead Institute for Sensitivity?

He slashed her an irritated glance. She was one of the most aggravating woman he'd ever run into—or more correctly, who'd ever run into him. "My boat is damaged, thanks to you," he said. "How cheerful do you expect me to be?"

He saw her flinch at the reminder. She opened her mouth to retort, closed it and turned away, muttering, "You don't have to be such a sorehead."

"Since you have the resident sore head, chances are I caught it from you." He winced at himself for that remark. He should have let the comment go. She was hurt and shaken up. People in her condition sometimes lashed out at any available target, occasionally the doctor. It didn't mean anything. When her lower lip began to tremble, he felt like a jerk for being short with her. It wasn't her fault the fog had rolled in and she'd gotten lost.

Apparently the boat she was sailing didn't belong to her. Marc had no idea what kind of problems that detail would cause. The faded jeans she wore were far from new. The white nylon sweater looked more discount than designer. On her left wrist she wore a white sweatband that was too lumpy to be covering only a wrist. She was probably protecting a watch or bracelet. Unless the jewelry was sprinkled with diamonds, she didn't appear to have a huge reservoir of ready cash for the repair of damaged catamarans.

Flipping off the lights, he carefully maneuvered around so the boat he towed followed in their slow wake. Glancing her way, he asked, "Who's cat is it?"

She slumped back in the tall, beige leather seat and took the handkerchief off her head, refolding it to find a fresh spot to soak up the oozing blood. Marc was impressed by her control. She wasn't a coward when it came to dealing with the sight of her own blood. He'd seen more than one senior medical student go woozy and sick when confronted by his own smashed finger or lacerated scalp. Maybe she really had set her own broken leg.

"Oh—it's just this guy's," she said, looking straight ahead. "I was practicing to enter the Habitat Race next weekend."

"What race?"

She glanced his way. The look was brief, but long enough for Marc to see the glitter of tears.

"The catamaran race to help build a new habitat for polar bears in the Portland zoo. The entry fees go toward building the habitat."

Marc had heard nothing about it, but he hadn't had time to visit a zoo in a decade. Even reading the daily paper was a luxury he could rarely indulge in. He watched her troubled profile for a long minute, then asked, "How's the head?"

She closed her eyes and slumped in the chair, appearing small and remote. "Peachy," she mumbled.

"You're not going to sleep, are you?" he asked, worried.

She flicked him an unhappy look. "Don't panic, doc. If I fall into a coma I'll make sure to sprawl to the deck so you'll be the first to know."

He felt an urge to chuckle at her wry wit, but stifled it, concentrating on maneuvering his cruiser through the fog. "Thanks. I'll listen for the thud."

Out of the corner of his eye, he could see her loll her head so she could see him better. She watched him with those silver eyes. Her quiet stare affected him strangely and a prickly restlessness surged through him. When he turned to look directly at her she didn't even blink, clearly unembarrassed to be caught staring.

Intrigued by this spitfire with so much passion and gall, he stared back. She had fuller lips than he'd first thought. Really great lips. If his hot-to-trot nurse had had lips like those—

"I was going to donate part of the grand prize money to the zoo." She heaved a sigh. "And use the rest to get to Java."

His unruly thoughts about her lips went up in heated smoke. "To where?"

She shrugged and shifted to face the windshield. "There's this orangutan preservation group I belong to that's trekking through Java in a couple of weeks. The money was to get me there."

Marc chuckled, incredulous. "You're kidding."

She turned. "Why would I kid about something like that?"

He lifted a brow to indicate his skepticism. "Even on the off chance that you won the race, why would you *do* something like that?"

She frowned. "Because the whole world is my backyard, doc, and I care about my backyard. Don't you?"

He studied her narrowed eyes and full lips, now thinned in idealistic defiance. After a drawn-out moment, he turned his full attention to docking his cruiser and its crippled floating baggage. A weird sense of frustration washed over him. Too bad such an attractive, spirited woman had to be a flighty loon.

Mimi had never expected to spend this evening sitting in a seaside cottage on some isolated island, having her head sewn up by a grumpy stick-in-the-mud who thought saving the Javanese orangutans was laughable.

She had to say one thing in the doctor's favor. He might be cynical about the plight of the world's endangered plants and animals and have a cranky bedside manner, but his touch was heavenly.

She chanced a peek at him as he stitched. His eyes and mind were focused on his work. With his expression so concentrated, he was yummy—in a somber, solid country-doctor way. Which was not to say that was necessarily a good thing. Somber, solid country doctors were a dull lot. Too narrowly focused on the here-and-now instead of tomorrow and the possibilities that made the world an exciting place to roam and explore.

Since she didn't have anything else to do, besides think about a needle puncturing her flesh, she decided it was better to concentrate on other things. Like the doc's eyes, for example. They were dazzling for a color as plain as brown.

She'd never thought of brown as erotic, but somehow Dr. Grouchy managed it. Maybe it was the long, curling coal-black lashes that made the difference. Whatever it was, those eyes had their effect. Even when he was frowning and barking orders, he had a way with those eyes. Maybe that's why she hadn't protested more than she had. Or maybe it was the wooziness and the fact that he'd had three heads there for a minute.

"All done," he said. "I doubt if there will even be a scar."

As his hands lifted away from her head she breathed a sigh that felt peculiarly like regret. He smelled good, even if there was a tinge of antiseptic in the mixture. She'd never found much fault with a man for smelling clean. And whatever else the doctor's scent included, it was one pleasant rush. Or maybe she'd just hit her head harder than she'd thought.

Instinctively, she lifted her hand to feel her wound, but was halted when he took her wrist. "Try not to touch it for a while," he cautioned. "Tomorrow you can shower as usual. In seven to ten days the sutures will dissolve on their own."

He lowered her arm to her thigh before letting go.

"Gee, thanks, doc," she quipped. "I would have never found my lap without your help."

"By the way," he asked, "What's under that sweatband?"

She looked down at it, then closed her hand over it fondly. "My most prized possessions." Tugging the band away she revealed two silver bracelets, brimming with charms. "My parents gave me these bracelets. The charms represent the places we've been."

"Hmmm." He turned away to take off his rubber gloves. "Tell me something," he said, tossing them in a trash container.

"I don't have insurance if that's what you're groping for. And you can't have my bracelets."

He faced her, his glance brief and narrowed. "Though I do have some patients who pay for my services in trade, Miss Baptiste, I don't want your bracelets." One corner of his mouth quirked, but she couldn't tell if the expression was amusement or contempt. "And my question wasn't about insurance, but it did involve money."

"I don't have any cash on me, either," she said. "Remember I told you I didn't need your help. You forced yourself on me."

"I'm a brute," he said quietly. "Now shut up for a second, and let me talk."

She lifted her arms in broad invitation. "Excuse me! Please! Talk! I keep forgetting that you sawbones are more important than we mere mortals!" She eyed him with all the animosity the accident had built up inside her. "Or is that more *egotistical*? I forget."

He settled on a nearby stool, crossing his arms over his broad chest. She took a quick second to scan him as he scowled at her. He wore beige trousers and a white polo shirt. Very conservative, very patient-friendly, very country-doctorly. Once inside his cottage he'd thrown on a white smock. Even with all his conventional professional trappings, he still looked less like a physician and more like a hunk with an attitude. "Did that remark about setting your own leg have any validity?"

She was taken aback by his arrogance. "Why? Do you actually believe the power to set a broken leg is the divine right of medical doctors?"

"Is that a no?"

"It's *not* a no! My parents were wildlife photographers. They traveled the world, and they wanted me with them. They home-schooled me and gave me experiences few other children get. Being on our own a lot we had to be resourceful." She straightened her shoulders, proud of her parents, world-famous in their field. "One day I was at camp doing some wash. I fell. By the time mother and father got back, I'd set my own leg."

He regarded her speculatively, and she sensed he was considering what she'd said, possibly even reluctantly deciding to believe her. She experienced a surge of gratification. He might not appreciate spontaneity or a vagabond lifestyle, but surely he appreciated courage and intelligence. She hiked her chin. "Well," she challenged. "Don't you have anything to say?"

Running a hand along his jaw, he nodded. "Yes. Will paying for repairs on that cat be a strain for you?"

She frowned at the unexpected question. "That's none of your business."

"I know, Miss Baptiste, and making it my business is the last thing I care to do. However, if you don't mind, humor me."

She minded, but shrugged. Much of the fight had gone out of her. She had a splitting headache; she was broke and she had nowhere to go. "I met this guy at a Clean Earth rally a couple of days ago and mentioned the race. He said he had a catamaran and if I wanted to enter I could use it. So he loaned it to me."

She felt a chill at the reminder, and ran her hands along her arms. *What was she going to do?* "The guy wasn't a close friend. I have no idea how he'll react when he sees the mess I made of his boat." Hearing the admission out loud made her stomach knot up. She was in trouble. The Java trip was definitely off. She'd have to find a temporary job to pay for the damage, plus earn the cost of transport to her next adventure—somewhere in the world—wherever and whatever that might be.

The tall, glowering doctor was quiet for what seemed like an hour. Mimi noticed the sound of a clock ticking and scanned the pine walls until she found it. A white-faced time-piece with a free-hanging pendulum hung between two windows draped in simple, blue-and-white checked cotton. They were in a small, tidy kitchen, all paneled in pine. Even the countertops were pine, worn and scarred from years of use. The place was as clean as a whistle. Even the blue woven throw rugs looked freshly laundered. Well, she supposed a doctor would be picky about cleanliness.

"Look, Miss Baptiste," he said, at last, drawing her gaze. He gritted his teeth. She could tell because the muscle in one cheek flexed. "I don't have time to beat around the bush. My nurse quit yesterday and I need help. If I pay for the repairs to your cat, will you work it off? Give me two weeks?"

She gaped, flummoxed. This possibility had never entered her mind. But a job was a job. Grumpy doctor or not, she needed work. She supposed this island was as good a place as any to spend a little time. It would be an experience to add to her growing list of adventures. She made a resigned face. "I suppose I could cook and do laundry. Whatever you need."

One brow rose. "I need a nurse."

She blinked, startled. "But—I'm—not..."

He shook his head. "Okay, call it an assistant. Somebody to go with me on rounds. And back here at the office, to fetch things, take appointments. I won't ask you to assist in brain surgery."

She swallowed and frowned, her thoughts strangely muddled. Maybe it was the head injury. She didn't seem to be able to think clearly.

He leaned toward her. "You need a job, right?"

She stared into narrowed eyes, so intent she could almost feel their heat. Uncharacteristically mute, she could only nod.

"I need help and I think you'll do." He sat back, his expression far from happy. "Give me two weeks of your time and I'll make sure the catamaran is put back in mint condition. What do you say?"

"It—it wasn't in mint condition to begin with," she murmured, stalling.

"Okay, it'll be better than it was," he said. "So sue me."

She shot him a glance. "You don't have to bite my head off. I was just making a point."

He ran a hand through his hair. "Sorry." He inhaled and it looked like he was mentally counting to ten. "What do you say?"

Did she really want to be stuck on a dinky island for two whole weeks, practically lashed to the hip of this testy sawbones? *Do you have a choice, Mimi*? she asked herself morosely. It could take her several days to find other work, and even then there was no guarantee the money would be decent. What he offered was way above and beyond what she'd get anyplace else. It would take at least a couple of thousand dollars to repair that catamaran. She looked at him with high suspicion. "That's a lot of money, doc. You must pay your assistants well."

"It's hard for us ax murderers to keep good help," he said, his expression perfectly serious.

The deadpan wisecrack surprised Mimi. She fought back an urge to grin. Weighing him with a critical stare, she crossed her arms before her. "Um-hmm." He was awfully good-looking, so it was pretty evident the trouble was his rotten disposition. Considering her experience with him so far, she would bet her last dollar that spending two weeks with him would be any sane person's limit.

She had a sudden thought. Though she needed a job really quickly that paid *really* well, really badly, she decided she'd only stay on one, tough condition. "Besides paying for the cat repairs, I'll need money to get where I'm going. Will you pay for that?" She wondered whether she'd be more relieved if he agreed or told her to go jump. She was asking one heck of a lot.

He eyed heaven. "Where are you going?"

"I—I don't know. Java's probably out." She shrugged. "I guess I'll decide that when the time comes."

"Excellent planning."

Mimi wasn't fooled by the positive remark. She could tell by his tone he thought she was a nomadic nutcase. She'd bet anything the idea of not knowing where he'd be next month was as foreign to him as—as skinny dipping. Well, that was just dandy with her. Disapproval coming from a narrow-minded sourpuss like him was a compliment. "Make it three weeks," he said, "and I'll throw in airfare to wherever you want to go."

Her heart dropped. "Three weeks?"

"It's not death row," he said. "Do we have a deal?"

Sweeping a strand of her hair off her face, she looked away. In the ten years since her parents had died, she'd had plenty of temporary jobs and knew how hard they were to come by—at least the ones that paid more than subsistence wages. She doubted she could do better and grimaced. "I guess."

When she glanced back at him, he was checking his watch. "Are you hungry?"

His abrupt change of subject startled her. She hadn't eaten much today, and though her pride was stung by his invalidation of everything she was or stood for, she wasn't stupid enough to cut off her nose to spite her face. "I could eat," she admitted.

"Can you cook?" He slid off the stool to stand beside her chair.

"Of course." His towering nearness unsettled her, so she pushed up from the little kitchen table. *What difference does it make if he validates you, Mimi?* she counseled inwardly. *You're completely capable, and what he thinks isn't important*! ''I can cook over hot volcanic ash if I have to.''

He had shrugged out of his white coat and was hanging it on a hook beside the door when her comment made him glance at her over his shoulder. His brows knit slightly, and she had a feeling he didn't believe her. ''That won't be necessary. I have a stove.''

She decided this staid, provincial MD needed a little loosening up. ''Too bad,'' she kidded. ''Where's the adventure in cooking on a stove?''

He lounged against the counter, resting the heels of his hands on the pine surface. His slouch was so utterly natural and sexy the sight was disconcerting. She decided there were movie-star hunks who stood in front of mirrors for hours, practicing but failing to look so cavalierly male. Belatedly, she realized his expression held a trace of disapproval. ''So life to you is just one big adventure, is it?''

The way he said it sent a ripple of irritation along her spine. ''Life *is* an adventure, doc. You have to make the most of the time you have.'' The muscle in his cheek flexed again. He was clenching. ''Do you have a problem with that?''

"Not at all," he said. "As long as you don't run out on me before your three weeks are up."

She lifted her chin. His assumption that she was some kind of two-faced weasel who wouldn't keep her promise infuriated her. "If I say I'll stay, I'll stay."

"Then I have your word?" he asked, not missing a beat.

She stared at him, doing a little teeth-grinding of her own. "Can I trust you to repair the cat and give me the airfare you agreed to?"

His gaze narrowed, and Mimi could tell the good doctor wasn't accustomed to having his word challenged. "Touché, Miss Baptiste," he said, gravely.

"So we're agreed," she retorted. "You do your part, and I'll stay three weeks. But not a day longer."

CHAPTER TWO

MIMI and the doctor shared a long, explicit glare.

Mixed somewhere in her anger and frustration she felt a tingle of satisfaction. It didn't take a psychic to see that Doctor Charm was as annoyed about this arrangement as she.

A knocking sound brought an end to their staring contest. "Excuse me," he muttered, striding out of the kitchen toward the cottage's front door. Mimi was curious to see who might need a doctor at this hour, so she ambled through the kitchen and into the dining area. Leaning against the round table, she watched the doctor stalk toward the front entrance.

The only hint that the living room before her doubled as a waiting area was a wooden desk that sat beside the front door. Behind it a couple of tall wood filing cabinets stood against the side wall. Otherwise, the place looked like any other seaside cottage's living room.

When Marc swung the door wide, a white ball of fluff bounded inside, barking and wagging its stubby tail so hard it looked like it might split into two little puffs. Right behind the tiny creature came an attractive woman with shoulder-length auburn hair and a riot of freckles dancing across her pretty face.

"Hi," she said, giving the doctor a hug. "I saw your lights and figured you'd want Foo Foo back."

Marc returned the hug and kissed the newcomer's forehead. "The fog must be lifting."

"The wind's picked up..." Her sentence trailed away when she noticed Mimi. "Oh—I didn't realize you had a patient."

At the same moment, the white fluff-ball noticed Mimi and ran to her as though she was its long-lost mama. Leaping and barking and wagging, it greeted her with considerably more enthusiasm than Mimi felt.

"Hush, Foof!" the woman called. "You're not supposed to bother the patients."

"She's not a patient, Susan." Marc clasped the woman about the shoulders and guided her into the room. "She's my temporary assistant.

I found her tonight." He indicated Mimi with a gesture. "Susan Merit, Miss...Baptiste."

Mimi felt a twinge at the obvious fact that he couldn't recall her first name. It was odd, though, that the twinge had begun some time before he'd spoken her name. Surely the fact that he had a wife didn't bother her. She didn't even like the aggravating sourpuss.

When she realized Marc and Susan had neared, she belatedly held out a hand. "It's Mimi. Mimi Baptiste. Nice to meet you."

Susan took her hand and squeezed, then glanced askance at Marc. "I know it's hard to find help, sweetie, but bashing women over the head is just a little illegal."

He grinned at Susan, and Mimi was struck by the sight. His smile transformed his features, making his good looks devastating. She swallowed hard. Maybe it was lucky the doctor was basically a grouch. Maybe he'd learned the hard way that he *had* to be a grouch, at least with female patients. Mimi decided his smiles were almost too stimulating to cope with, even fully clothed. What sort of chaos might one of those rakish grins cause if flashed during a physical exam?

"Very funny, Susan." He squeezed the

woman's shoulder affectionately before dropping his arm to his side.

The dog jumped up on Mimi, yapping, clearly begging to be picked up. Tiny and pure white, the animal was probably a poodle but without the traditional cut.

"Down, Foof," Marc commanded. "Time for dinner." The ball of fuzz dropped its forepaws to the floor, danced around in a circle, then dashed into the kitchen.

Marc turned to the auburn-haired woman. "How's Kyle?"

Susan smiled, a bright blush spreading across her cheeks. "He's the sweetest little boy on earth." She reached up and touched Marc's cheek. "Thank you for that darling baby." She cleared her throat, as though fighting emotion. Her smile trembled, then brightened and became teasing. "Come on up and see us, sometime."

He winked. "It's a date."

Susan turned to Mimi. "Don't let this ogre work you too hard. And don't let him forget to eat, okay?" She wrapped her arms about his waist and gave him a displeased look. "You're too thin."

Marc's laughter was rich, filling the room

with an unexpected warmth. "Will the nagging never end?"

She pecked his cheek. "Okay, okay, I'm going. Foo Foo was a delight as usual, but I'm afraid once Kyle is old enough to toddle around, he's going to steal that dog away from you. She's pretty fond of him already. Thinks he's her baby."

"If Kyle takes Foof away, you have to grant me visitation rights," he kidded.

"Ha!" Susan countered. "Like you'd take time to visit." She disengaged herself from Marc. When she met Mimi's gaze again, her smile dimmed. "If Marc didn't bash you, then how did you hurt your head?"

Mimi felt peculiarly impish. "Oh, but he did!" She shot him a taunting look. "It was a clear case of piracy on the high seas. First he rammed me to disable my boat, then he kidnapped me. It was horrible."

Marc's smile became a trifle jaundiced. "Two funny women in the same room. I'm blessed."

Susan gave him a look. "In all the time I've known you, Marc, I've never suspected you had this buccaneering streak. "

"Well, I've witnessed his dark side," Mimi said before Marc could do more than open his mouth. "To add insult to injury, he insists I work for him for three whole weeks to pay for repairing the damage to *both* boats!"

Susan squinted at Marc. "You fiend." She stepped away from him and placed her hands on her hips. "Under that wholesome doctor's facade I find out you're into assault, kidnapping and blackmail."

Marc's glance went from Susan to Mimi then back to Susan. "You've found me out. I'm a regular Renaissance felon." His grin was teasing and aimed at Susan, but it had an effect on Mimi and she didn't like it one bit. This doctor had none of the attributes she wanted in a man. Well, maybe a few of the basics—like brains and looks and great teeth—but not the important ones.

"Dr. Blackbeard, huh?" Susan laughed. "I'm sorry, Marc, but I don't believe it. Not from our incorruptible Dr. Merit." Facing Mimi, she said, "Did he tell you why his last nurse left?"

Mimi shook her head. She'd assumed it was because his growling attitude left a lot to be desired.

"Let's not—"

"*Because*," Susan cut in over Marc's objection, "he wouldn't play nursie-doctor games with her—if you get my meaning."

Startled by the sexual innuendo, Mimi glanced at Marc. Though his face showed a deep summer tan, his features still managed to go a shade darker. "Thanks, Suze," he muttered. "I might have forgotten to mention that."

Susan's grin was playful as she touched Mimi's hand. "He's an uncompromising goody-goody, but we love him anyway."

Mimi cast the doctor a curious look. The flush beneath his tan exhibited a captivating hint of vulnerability. He might be a bear, but he was cute when he was embarrassed. Plainly his wife didn't have any doubts about his fidelity if she felt comfortable teasing him about the women who would be his lovers, if only he'd slip off his white charger.

"Go away, Suze," he grumbled. "I think I hear the baby calling you."

She laughed. "I love you, too, sweetie." Glancing at her watch, she added, "It is time for Kyle's bedtime bottle, but if you can hear him, you have better ears than Foof!" Giving Marc another fond pat on the cheek, she turned to Mimi. "We live up on the hill, so I hope I'll see you a lot. There aren't many women on the island, so I'm starved for girl talk." She turned away. "Assuming Cap'n Bligh gives you any time off."

"I'm not holding my breath," Mimi called after her, deciding the doctor used the cottage as an office and lived up the hill. Funny, she'd gotten the impression it was his home.

Susan's light laugh echoed in the room as the front door closed with a quiet click. Suddenly, Mimi found herself facing an unsmiling grouch, again. "I'll show you your room." He indicated the kitchen. "It's back there."

"Aye, aye, Cap'n." She struck a jaunty salute. "Lead the way, sir."

His expression stern, he headed into the kitchen. "Let me know where your things are. I'll have them delivered here tomorrow."

She'd been crashing on the sofa of a friend of an acquaintance, an elderly widow who rescued stray cats. The idea of sleeping without six or eight furry bodies curled on top of her seemed like quite a luxury. "Okay," she murmured, passing the fluff ball as it munched pellets from a bowl in the corner. "I'll write down the address."

"Fine." Adjacent to the back entrance, they rounded a corner into a short hallway. "This is where you'll sleep.'' He opened a door and flipped on a light, revealing a small, plainly furnished room. The place had a quaint, old-fashioned quality and looked clean enough to eat off any surface. ''The bath is on your right at the end of the hall. And this...'' he touched the knob on a door neighboring her own, ''...is my room.''

She went stock still and spun to confront him. ''*Your* room?''

His expression closed further. Apparently her question had come out more horrified than he was accustomed to hearing when describing the living arrangements. ''This is my house, Miss Baptiste. I thought you understood that.''

She experienced a rush of panic and didn't have a clue why. ''But—but don't you live on the hill?''

''No.'' He leaned against his door. ''I did once, but this is my home now.''

His marital status was none of Mimi's business, but she was surprised by the revelation. He and Susan seemed so—so friendly. She shrugged. ''That's too bad.''

''It is?''

She had looked away, trying to get a grip

on what she was feeling. "So you're separated?"

"What?"

"From your wife and baby." She met his gaze, somehow unable to do otherwise.

He crossed his arms before him. "My wife and baby?"

"Do you have a hearing problem, doc?" She waved toward the living room. "Susan—Mrs. Merit, that is—and your baby, Kyle. They live on the hill, but you live here?" She frowned in thought. The doctor was a handsome brute. No woman would reject him because of his looks. He could be extremely ill-tempered, but he'd been charming with Susan. No doubt he was trying to get back into her good graces after some transgression. "Was it the long hours, or too many amorous nurses—or what—that split you up?" She wondered at herself for feeling the need to know.

He watched her with a curious expression. "Excuse me?"

How could a man be a doctor and be this dense? She heaved an exasperated sigh. "Why don't you and Susan live together?"

"Why don't...?" His lips quirked. "Oh."

"Oh?" How annoying—what kind of answer was *oh*? "Are you telling me it's none of my business?'' she asked, well aware that it wasn't. She supposed, growing up in the wild, both her parents and her environment unique to say the least, she hadn't become as proficient in the subtleties of tact as those who'd grown up in more conventional situations. Sometimes she asked outlandish questions. People were free to answer them or not. Surprisingly, many did.

''You're right. It isn't your business, Miss Baptiste,'' he said. ''However, it's no secret why Susan and I aren't living together, so you'd find out soon enough, anyway.''

She waited, watching his eyes. They had a powerful pull, and right now, they also contained a suspicious twinkle.

''It's just a guess,'' he said, ''but I don't think her husband would approve.''

''Her hus—'' Mimi was confused. ''But I thought she was Mrs. Merit?''

''She is,'' he said, matter-of-factly. ''She's Mrs. Jake Merit, my sister-in-law.''

Mimi was totally bewildered now. Even somewhat horrified. ''Then why did she thank *you* for the baby?'' As soon as the words were out of her mouth she regretted it. ''*No! No!*'' She threw up her arms, gesturing in the negative. "Never mind. Some things I *don't* want to be my business."

His lips twisted wryly. "Not enough things, apparently." Pushing away from the wall, he added, "But for the sake of your shocked sensibilities, Susan thanked me because I was instrumental in the adoption of their baby."

Mimi's lips opened in a silent gasp. She felt stupid. No, she felt more than stupid. She had an overwhelming urge to sew her lips together. "Makes sense," she murmured.

"I'll sleep better knowing you think so." His sarcasm stung, and she winced as he turned toward the kitchen. "About dinner," he said. "What do you feel like?"

"An idiot," she mumbled.

He passed her, heading around the corner. Mimi couldn't be sure, but she had a sneaky suspicion he was fighting a grin. The bum. He hadn't been dense or hard of hearing! He'd enjoyed watching her jump to the wrong conclusion. He thought it was hilarious that she'd made a perfect fool of herself. Obviously life on the island was so boring he had to get his kicks flustering people.

She took several restorative breaths before she worked up the nerve to follow him. When she entered the kitchen, he was placing a pot on the stove. "How about spaghetti?" he asked, without turning.

"Well..." She'd lost her appetite, but humiliated or not she supposed she should eat.

He shifted to glance at her, his brows knitting. "Don't tell me it's not enough of an adventure, that you'd rather go out and bring down a wildebeest with your bare hands." He turned away. "It's late, I'm tired and we're a little low on wildebeests at the moment, so it's spaghetti or nothing."

Her humiliation mutated into aggravation. "I didn't say *anything*, doc. Spaghetti's fine." She headed to the stove and yanked the pot from him. "Go gnaw on a table leg. I'll call you when it's ready."

She eyed him with high irritation as his expression went from annoyed to perplexed then finally to weary. "I'm sorry, Miss Baptiste." He shook his head. "It's been a long day."

She felt a weird urge to smooth the shiny hank of hair off his creased brow, but she kept her hands clamped firmly on the pot handle. Okay, so she got a little fluttery and feminine around him. She wasn't dead, just not interested in going all gooey over a man who wasn't a globe-trotter, like her. Letting herself get lost in a pair of brown eyes was foolish, only leading to grief when it was time to move on. With a rankled clearing of her throat, she escaped to the sink. "Yeah, well I've been eating bon bons all day, doc, so I'm fresh as a daisy. Except for the gaping head wound, of course. Now *go*!"

She turned on the water, but her senses remained riveted on the doctor. She didn't want her senses riveted there, but they insisted on it. That was another annoying quality about Dr. Marc Merit. He was impossible to ignore, snarling or smiling—or even standing completely still behind her back.

She couldn't see him, didn't hear him, so she assumed he hadn't moved. When she turned off the water, she heard the sound of the refrigerator door opening. Glancing around she saw Marc remove a package of hamburger. "What are you doing?" she asked, deciding the man didn't take orders at all well.

He made brief eye contact, then walked to the stove. "Tomorrow, being Sunday, is a day off unless there's an emergency. You'll have time to get settled in and acquainted with the island." He opened a low cabinet door beside the stove and drew out a frying pan. "Tonight,

I'll leave a T-shirt and some socks in the bathroom for you to put on after your bath.''

She was surprised by his offer, then realized she probably looked pretty straggly. "Thanks." Lugging the pot to the stove, she placed it on a burner and turned on the gas.

Marc dumped the meat into the saucepan and began to break it up with a cooking fork. The tension between them was almost palpable. Mimi didn't know when she'd been more aware of a man—or more disturbed by one. She was as unhappy about being stuck on an island with him as she was miserable about missing the Java trek.

If she forced herself to look at the situation objectively, this whole mess wasn't the doctor's fault. It was hers. She tended to go off half-cocked, and not think things through. Borrowing the boat from somebody she hardly knew then sailing it into a fog bank had been two of those half-cocked notions that were coming back to bite her. Hard. "Look, doc..." she made herself face him. Maybe she owed him an apology. *Maybe*? an annoying little voice scoffed.

He didn't glance her way, but kept breaking up the meat as it started to sizzle.

"Marc?" she said, almost too quietly to hear. Apologizing wasn't her strongest suit.

He stopped and glanced her way, a brow going up in question.

She shrugged, feeling rotten. She was tired too, and she had a splitting headache, but right was right. "I'm sorry about your boat." Breaking eye contact, she tugged the fork from his hand. "You're paying a lot of money to repair that cat, and I've said I'd work off the debt. So let me fix dinner."

He was big and solid, he smelled nice and he was too close for her peace of mind. If it weren't for his grouchiness and his "country doctor" lifestyle, he could easily be mistaken for the man she dreamed would one day come into her life. The man who would be to her what her dad had been to her mother. "Please?" she asked, miffed at herself for wasting even a second on silly romantic daydreams about Dr. Dutiful Of Sunnybrook Farm. "Just go."

His eyes narrowed for a heartbeat, then he shook his head. "No, Miss Baptiste. After working hours you're off the clock."

"That's ridiculous!" She nudged him with her hip. "Go! Shower! Nap! Punch holes in a wall! Do whatever it is you do to relax, and let me start paying for my keep!'' She nudged him harder. ''*Move it*!''

''Cut it out,'' he barked. ''I'm not some elephant stuck in a bog.''

She cast him a challenging glance. ''Are you sure about that, Doc?''

Restless and on edge, Marc rolled to his back. What in Hades was his problem? He was exhausted. His day began at five o'clock. It was now two in the morning, and all he could do was lie there and stare at the ceiling. Why couldn't he sleep? Usually he was unconscious before his head hit the pillow. Until tonight, he'd never realized Foo Foo snored.

He glanced at the tiny dog, curled in her bed. He watched her fuzzy little chest, highlighted by moonlight from the nearby window, expand with several doggie inhales. The sound she made was like a buzz saw grinding through bricks.

He closed his eyes and tried to ignore the roar. He knew a tiny animal like Foo Foo couldn't possibly make the kind of noise his brain insisted he was hearing. It was anatomically impossible. She'd have to be the size of a moose to be that loud. If he made himself face facts, it wasn't the snoring that was keeping him awake. It was the battering ram of a woman, Mimi Baptiste, who preyed on his mind.

The instant he'd spotted her on that blasted catamaran something had gotten screwed up in his head. His heart had swelled and his gut had sizzled. He'd never experienced any phenomenon like it, and the feeling alarmed him.

He'd come back to Merit Island because he'd decided doctoring in a big city wasn't for him. He missed home and friends and the laidback lifestyle he'd grown up with. He'd never had any urge to run the family emerald corporation and was glad Jake had taken over. Yet, Merit Island was a different matter. He'd tried to make a life somewhere else, but after a few years he'd come to realize this was where he was happiest; where he wanted to make his home.

He'd been fond of old Doc Fleet, and from the time he was twelve he'd gone on rounds with the physician whenever possible, getting to know folks on the surrounding islands. They'd become like an extended family to him. So when Doc Fleet and his wife retired to Montana to be closer to their grandchildren, Marc came back to settle down. His plan was to find a wife somewhere on one of the neighboring islets and build a family. Most of his friends were married with kids by now. At thirty-four, it was time he was too.

A doctor needed stability, both in his own character and in his home life. Mimi Baptiste was anything but stable. She was a will-o'-the-wisp, a pretty bird capriciously lingering for a time in his backyard. He dared not become enamored of her, for her nature was to fly away.

It annoyed him mightily that something inside him found her intriguing. It disturbed him that he'd felt more like a man than a doctor when he'd touched her hair, smelled the light scent of her skin. And it irked him almost beyond bearing that he was attracted to her free spirit and her sassy mouth. The impertinent way she called him doc and had prodded him bodily away from his own stove galled him— but just as strongly fostered a hunger to taste the passion she put into every word, look and gesture. He wanted to feel it, drink it in, make it a part of himself.

She was exasperating and exhilarating, bothersome and bewitching. *And she was not the woman for him*! Whatever quirky, wayward part of his psyche found her appealing had to be stomped out of existence. He promised himself to fight the attraction. Not get involved. Fending off Ursula and her kind was easy. It was bad business getting involved with employees. But the decision to remain indifferent to Mimi was harder fought. His body reacted wildly to her, giving no heed to the dictates of his brain.

He *wanted* this woman. He was afraid he might even fall for her if he didn't watch himself. And knowing the history of Merit men, they didn't fall lightly or lose a love without grievous personal consequence. His father, George, had never been the same after their mother died. And Jake? Well, he'd suffered the tortures of the damned for years and years over his lost Tatiana before Susan came along—Jake's "little freckle-faced angel" as he lovingly called his wife of two years.

Yes, Marc wanted a wife. He'd come home to find one. But *not* Mimi Baptiste. Not the hot-headed vagabond who would sooner be backpacking through a jungle with strangers and setting her own broken bones than making a home in some fixed location. *Get your mind off her, Merit, and go to sleep!*

Another long, rasping wheeze from Foo Foo's basket broke the quiet. Frustrated and annoyed with himself for his stubborn preoc-

cupation with such an inappropriate little spitfire, he rolled out of bed and padded to the
door. Stepping into the hallway, he slammed
bodily into someone.

The skulking night prowler mashed against
him wasn't very tall, and in certain strategic
areas, felt shockingly soft. Marc hoped like
hell it was a burglar.

CHAPTER THREE

MIMI couldn't see very well in the dimness of the hallway, but her sense of touch revved into high gear. If she knew anything about anything, she knew she'd just smashed into a very solid male. Her lips, her breasts, her—well, most of her body—recorded varying anatomical sections of his masculinity with equal measures of shock and gusto. A muffled curse somewhere above her head told her the doctor-in-residence was simply ecstatic about their late-night encounter.

"This time you really did run into me, doc," she muttered, provoked by his undisguised distaste. She wished she could be as irritated by the feel of his body as he clearly was by hers. She laid her hands against his bare chest, registering how warm and sturdy he felt. Her palms tingled at the contact with a liberal scattering of crisp hair. She even detected his heartbeat and registered the fact that it was a little fast. Even so, it didn't have a chance if it planned to race against her own which had taken off in a sprint the instant they'd made contact and was miles away by now.

He smelled even nicer up close and she winced. This was not productive, not in her best interests and, unfortunately, not a rendezvous she would easily forget. Pressing against him she was startled to feel resistance and noticed for the first time that he'd wrapped his arms about her. "Uh-you can let go," she murmured, her voice vaguely breathy, "I won't faint. I've had worse blows—"

"—trying on men?" Marc interrupted curtly.

His gruff question astonished her and her glance sprang to his face. His clenched jaws and narrowed gaze came as no surprise. "I was going to say, getting rammed by seagoing sawbones," she retorted. Her love life, whether she had one or not, was none of his business. "But let's go with yours, doc. It's much more colorful."

His nostrils flared at her gibe, but he didn't speak.

She slid her hands down his chest, wondering why she chose to do that instead of merely lifting them away. The rational portion of her brain lagged a beat or two behind as she skimmed her fingers along his forearms until she reached his wrists. Sadly, this move was another of her half-baked ideas. In this position, with her hands behind her, she had to press her breasts even more intimately into him.

Mimi wore only the oversized T-shirt he'd provided for her to sleep in, and it was proving too thin to keep the texture of his chest from registering against her. The sensation stirred something in her that was troubling, even disturbing.

She didn't like feeling anything for him but righteous anger. How dare he assume that because she was a free spirit, she was also less than discriminating when it came to men! Such narrow-minded arrogance hurt her feelings and made her mad. Swallowing to steady her voice, she allowed her ire to help disengage his hands from the small of her back. "If that's your idea of a come-on, doc, it needs work," she said as evenly as she could. "My head is pounding, so if you'll excuse me, I have a date with your medicine cabinet and an aspirin."

Peculiarly light-headed, she lurched away, thrusting out an arm to steady herself with the wall. A hand grasped her outstretched wrist, halting her.

"Look, Miss Baptiste," he said, sounding less gruff. "Forgive me. I wasn't—quite awake." Tugging, he compelled her to turn toward him. "I have something in my office that will help your headache." Indicating the kitchen, he squeezed her wrist briefly as though coaxing without words. "I could eat. How about you?" He smiled, the act brief and forced, but influential, none the less. Mimi hated to think what might happen if the doctor ever directed a full-fledged grin in her direction.

Lifting her shoulders in a resigned shrug, she nodded. "Okay. Maybe I could eat a couple of wildebeest on whole wheat."

His eyes widened a fraction, and Mimi thought she saw the bare beginnings of actual humor. "You make the sandwiches and I'll get the medicine."

She was amazed at herself for not pulling out of his grasp as he led her into the kitchen and flipped on the overhead light. She flinched, the sudden brightness blazing and painful. "Ouch!"

Marc glanced at her, then flipped off the light. "You don't do electricity much?"

"Not five-thousand-watt bulbs," she quipped, though she knew the blame lay with her throbbing head.

"I think I can come up with more head-ache-friendly wattage." Releasing her, he went to a cabinet and retrieved a couple of chunky candles and a book of matches. In a few seconds a soft twinkle illuminated the room from the center of the kitchen table. "Is that better?" he asked, facing her.

He stood there in the half light, looking rough-hewn and gilded in a pair of low-riding, draw-string pajama bottoms. He made such a stirring picture, she wasn't sure if *yes* was a meaningful enough word. Not to mention the fact that such a masculine spectacle wasn't helping her head. She nodded, removing her gaze to the less inflammatory view of the refrigerator. "Er—thanks."

"I'll just be a minute."

"Take your time," she mumbled. The medicine he was getting had better be strong enough to drop a horse. She was afraid the stimulation of running bodily into him, then having to observe his broad chest and muscular torso in flickering candlelight—well, it might not be the sort of experience that aided and abetted peace of mind.

"Don't think about it, Mimi," she muttered under her breath as she fished around in the refrigerator. "Don't look directly at him. Fix the sandwiches. Take the pill and go!"

When Marc returned, Mimi was working at the countertop next to the refrigerator. Her back was to him. The shirt he'd loaned her hit half way between her hips and knees. The white sport socks were crushed down around her ankles. Her blond, tousled hair fell to just past her shoulders. She looked like somebody's little girl dressed in her daddy's shirt and socks. No. Not a little girl, Marc amended. Even in the candlelight he could detect vague shadows that hinted at womanly curves, curves he had recently found to be tormentingly real. An awkward stab in his gut made him flinch. *You're a doctor, man!* he warned inwardly. *Act like one!* Clearing his throat to announce his presence, he approached her, working to present his best professional demeanor.

As he neared, she picked up two plates and turned. Each dish held a sandwich which had been sliced diagonally. "Two wildebeest sandwiches coming up." When she saw what he held, her expression closed. "What's that?"

He lifted it. "A hypodermic. This will work faster."

She made a face and slipped by him to deposit the plates on the table. Marc didn't miss the fact that she placed them at opposite ends. "I thought it was going to be a pill, doc." She turned to face him.

He lifted a brow in challenge. "I thought you were the woman who set her own bones. Surely a little needle can't bother you."

She crossed her arms. "You've already stabbed me with a needle a bunch of times, today. Aren't you getting tired of using me for a pin cushion?"

"I'm fighting it," he said, surprised at himself. Doctoring wasn't anything to kid about.

She eyed him ruefully, then reluctantly uncrossed her arms and rolled up one sleeve. "Okay. Have a party."

He liked her spunk. When he reached her, she gave him a petulant look. "I fixed you a great sandwich and look at the way you repay me."

"You'll feel better. Are you allergic to any pain relievers?"

"Strawberries."

He felt an urge to smile but mastered it. "Luckily, I hardly ever use strawberries as a pain killer."

She grimaced. "Oh, did you say pain killers? Then the answer's no—at least I don't think so."

"What do strawberries do to you?" He pulled his gaze from hers and got to business swabbing alcohol on a small area on her upper arm.

"I break out in hives and itch."

"Hmm."

She laughed.

Puzzled, he glanced at her. "What was that for?"

She shook her head. "Nothing. You just sounded very doctorly there with that *hmm.* Do you learn that in doctor college? When you don't know what to say you just go *hmm*?"

He grinned, then caught himself and turned back to his work, giving her the shot. "I know what to say, Miss Baptiste."

"Oh? What's that?"

"Don't eat strawberries."

She giggled again, the sound rippling along his spine. The sensation was strange and exciting, one he'd never experienced before.

He glanced at her face. Her eyes were closed. "All done." She peeked at him and he held up the empty syringe. "That wasn't so bad, was it?"

She turned away and pulled out a chair. "Let's just try not to make a habit of it, okay?" Plunking herself down, she waved toward his sandwich. "So eat, doc."

After disposing of the syringe, he took the chair opposite hers and glanced at his food. "Wildebeest, huh?"

"Absolutely." She placed her elbows on the table and rested her chin on her hands. "On whole wheat."

Curious as to what the sandwich really contained, he lifted the top piece of bread off one wedge and was surprised to see a glob of cold spaghetti and meat sauce smashed between the slices. He looked at her in disbelief. "You made me a cold spaghetti sandwich?"

She nodded, her smile a little lopsided. "How's your headache?"

Pursing her lips, she scrunched up her face, seeming to consider his question with great care. After a long minute, she whispered, "Pretty cool."

This time when he fought a smile, he lost. "That's nice." Miss Baptiste was having a rapid and strong reaction to the pain medication.

She reinstated her lopsided smile. "Say, doc?"

He put the bread back on top of the congealed spaghetti. "Yes?"

Her brows knit slightly. "Don't worry."

He leaned closer. She was whispering now, and he wasn't sure he'd heard her right. "Don't worry?"

"Uh-huh."

"About what, Miss Baptiste?"

She canted toward him, placing the flats of both hands on the table. Her fingertips nearly touched the candles. "I won't chase you around your office."

"What?" Surely he hadn't heard her right.

She lifted a finger to her lips and shushed him. "You're very cute, Doc, but you're not my type."

He blinked and sat back. The fact that he wasn't her type was certainly no news flash, but her bluntness startled him. Clearly she was feeling no pain. How ironic that her whispered vow was painful for him. Not that he'd wanted her to chase him around the office, but the idea of, well, a little mutual chasing had crept into his thoughts. "I—uh—appreciate your frankness."

"It's like this, Doc," she whispered, "I won't be here long, and no matter what you think, I don't jump into the sack for sport."

He clenched his teeth. Yes, he had made a crack like that, hadn't he? Leaning forward, he started to speak, then saw the glimmer of tears in her eyes. That stopped him dead, his mouth open.

"You don't like me, doc." It wasn't a question.

He cleared his throat. "I—of course I like you, Miss Baptiste." *I don't want to like you,* he went on mentally, *and I'll be relieved when you're gone.* "If it makes you feel better, you're not my type, either."

She sniffed, her expression remaining somber. "That's lucky, doc," she whispered, then curled her arms around her plate and laid her head squarely on her sandwich. "Lucky..." she murmured.

"Miss Baptiste?" he asked softly

No response.

She'd fallen asleep. Marc watched her for a minute. Her hair glistened in the soft light. Her hands lay just on the other side of the candles, quiet and graceful. The charm bracelets circling her left wrist glittered, reminding him of her eyes. With a bemused shake of his head, he rose to his feet and blew out the candles. Though he wasn't crazy about the necessity, he moved to her side of the table and gently lifted her into his arms.

Funny, she seemed awfully light. He could have sworn she was more woman than this small package he held in his arms. Instinctively, she snuggled in the harbor of his embrace, hugging him close. Her lips rested against the hollow of his throat, moist, warm and provocative.

His gut clenched and he reminded himself he was a physician and, at the moment, she was a patient. Tomorrow she would be an employee. Any amorous feelings she might arouse in him had better be permanently shelved, because Mimi Baptiste was absolutely right about one thing. He wasn't her type, and she wasn't his. It was good to have that out in the open, and lucky they were in agreement.

Blowing out a long exhale from between clenched teeth, he carried the warm and willowy nomad to her room. "Yeah," he muttered, trying to keep his mind on a professional plane. "Damn lucky."

* * *

Mimi felt refreshed and rested, her headache completely gone. Sitting up in bed, she stretched. She didn't know when she'd had such a good night's sleep. The first twinge of the day wasn't due to any physical pain, but to the fact that she became aware of where she was.

"Right," she mumbled. "I'm Dr. Grumpy's bond slave." With an accepting sigh, she jumped out of bed. "No sense crying over spilt catamarans." She noticed a familiar army-green duffel leaning against the wall beside her door. Curious, she padded to it and loosened the drawstrings.

She stared down at her own things, astonished. How did they get here? Planning to find out how the doctor could materialize her things practically out of thin air, she pulled a knit top and a pair of clean jeans from the bag and threw them on. After dashing to the bathroom to brush her teeth and comb her hair she went in search of her host-slash-jailer.

The quest wasn't a long one, since he sat casually at the kitchen table, sipping a mug of coffee and reading a newspaper. His feet rested on one of the chairs, legs crossed at the ankles. He wore hiking boots, jeans and a comfortable-looking chocolate-brown shirt, the sleeves rolled up to his elbows. Little Foo Foo had curled her negligible bulk beside his chair.

Very domesticated scene, she thought. *A man and his powder puff.*

He glanced up. "Hi." The greeting was pleasant enough, though not accompanied with a smile.

"Morning, doc." She ambled in. "What would you like for breakfast?"

He lowered his mug to the table. "It's two o'clock in the afternoon, Miss Baptiste. Thanks, but I've just finished lunch."

His pronouncement came as a blow. "Two?" She stared. "No! It can't be!"

He folded his newspaper and placed it on the table. "In Hawaii it's only eight, if that makes you feel any better." He pushed up from the chair. "Susan brought us some lunch." He took his mug to the counter and refilled it from a half-full pot. "Your plate is in the refrigerator." He glanced at her. "Would you like coffee?"

Frowning she nodded absently. "But how could I have slept...?" She had a thought. "It was that medicine you gave me. It knocked me for a loop."

His lips quirked slightly. "One of the possible side effects is drowsiness.'' He returned to the table and placed a mug of steaming coffee at her place. ''But since it was the middle of the night, I didn't think you'd mind.''

Upset and not sure at whom, she opened the refrigerator and spied a plate covered with cling wrap. ''Is it this dish wrapped in plastic?''

''If it looks like shrimp salad, it is.''

She took it to the table, seating herself opposite him, where silverware and a blue-and-white checked napkin had been set out. ''Susan brought this?''

Marc turned his chair to face her and folded his forearms on the table. ''Uh-huh.''

She felt restless under his direct gaze and busied herself taking the cling wrap off the salad. ''It was nice of her to make us lunch.''

''She didn't make it, but it was nice of her to bring it.''

Mimi glanced at him, confused.

''Usually one of the kitchen staff brings it. But Susan was anxious to visit with you.'' He took a sip of his coffee. ''We're invited for dinner.''

Mimi picked up her fork, but his last words halted her in the middle of stabbing a fat piece of shrimp. ''What?''

"Dinner. You know, the meal that comes several hours after lunch?"

She made a face. "I understand the progression. Even *I* eat." She took a bite of the salad. After swallowing, she added, "But I thought I was here to work. How am I going to pay my debt if you let me sleep all day and Susan does the work? What am I supposed to do?"

"I told you Sunday is a day off, barring emergencies. Susan knows that, so she invited us over. I accepted, figuring you'd be hungry."

She eyed him levelly. His expression wasn't quite sunny, but he wasn't glowering at her for a change. Something registered in her brain that she hadn't absorbed until now. "What did you mean by 'usually one of the kitchen staff brings it'?"

His lips twisted in a sardonic grin. "I was under the impression your first language was English, Miss Baptiste. Which words didn't you understand?"

She leaned toward him. "I'll have you know, *besides* English, I speak four languages fluently. One of them being Bantu, the language of the Swahili and the official language of Tanzania. I also speak French, German and

Spanish. How many languages do you speak, Doctor?''

"*Besides* English, a little Latin." He relaxed back in his chair. "And to answer your question, it's a big place."

Susan couldn't remember the question. "What is?"

"Where Susan lives."

"Oh." She remembered asking now, but was still perplexed. "She lives in a place that needs twenty people to take care of it? What is it, a hotel?"

He brushed a stray lock of hair off his forehead. "You haven't seen the residence on the hill, have you?"

She was startled by his query. "It was foggy when you dragged me kicking and screaming ashore, remember?"

With a thoughtful nod, he stood. "I remember the fog, but I can't recall the kicking and screaming part." He walked to her side and held out a hand as though he expected her to take it. "Come on."

She gaped at his extended fingers for a couple of heartbeats, then regained her senses. *She was not taking this man's hand*! "I'm eating." To reinforce her statement, she took a big bite.

"It'll just take a second, Miss Baptiste."
He lowered his arm, seeming to think better
of the hand-holding idea. "I just want you to
look out the front door."

He turned away, as though expecting her to
follow. She watched him disappear into the
dining room. Deciding he couldn't make her
jump because it was his whim, she stabbed
another piece of shrimp and ate it.

"Miss Baptiste?" he called. "I thought you
were in a lather to pay your debt. If following
me to the front door goes beyond your willingness to comply, perhaps you'd rather fork
over the cash you owe me and be on your
way?"

The bite of shrimp stuck in her throat and
she coughed. He made a painful point. What
was she doing, sitting there like some kind of
queen bee when she'd just ranted that she
should be working? Didn't she listen to herself when she ranted? What was her problem,
refusing to follow him to the front door?

Okay, if she had to explain her reluctance,
it was a knee-jerk reaction to her unwilling-
ness to hold his hand. She had to get herself
under control! "Mimi," she mumbled, "get
your priorities straight. Go ahead and avoid
the doctor's touch, but for heaven's sake, do

what he asks of you until you stumble over a few thousand dollars of ready cash.''

Pushing up from her chair, she headed after him. ''Did you want me, doc?'' she called, hoping a joke would ease the tension. ''Why didn't you just say so?''

She entered the dining room and saw him. He'd propped a lean hip on the desk beside the front door. With a lazy nod, he stood. ''Thanks, I'll try to remember that.''

He opened the door and motioned that she precede him onto the veranda. He walked to the rail, his boots resounding on the wood, and waved toward the gradual rise of land before them. ''There it is.''

Off in the distance Mimi spied a three-story stone-and-timber manor house, the like of which she'd only seen once before, when she and her parents had traveled through one particularly affluent section of the English countryside. She could only imagine the spectacular view from the summit, overlooking not only the Atlantic, but a gleaming pond dotted with gliding swans.

Radiating out in all directions were acres of gardens and velvety grass. On this lovely June afternoon, thousands upon thousands of plantings were in vivid bloom. Here and there, marble statuary glinted amid the riot of color. Scattered throughout the man-made paradise towered ancient maples, oaks and firs, offering shady, welcoming retreats. Mimi loved nothing more than reading in the shade of a big palm, baobab, redwood—whatever was available in the corner of the world where she happened to be.

"Beautiful trees," she breathed.

A deep chuckle brought her out of her mental wanderings and she glanced at the tall man beside her. His grin was accompanied by a dubious look. "Thanks, Nature Girl, but I was showing you the house."

She blinked. "Oh—of course. It's nice. That's where Susan lives?"

He turned away from the view and leaned against the railing. "Susan, Jake and their baby, Kyle, live there, as well as our father, George, and around two dozen servants."

Mimi absorbed the statement and nodded, glancing past Marc at the mansion. "Your brother and your father live there?"

"Yes."

"And you don't?" She pinned him with a narrowed look. "It's pretty bad when you're too grouchy for your own family to deal with, doc." She tisk-tisked, shaking her head. "I bet you had to take remedial Bedside Manner before they'd give you your diploma.''

"I'm not grouchy," he said, glowering at her.

She lifted her chin. "Right, and I'm not standing here with forty stitches in my head.''

"Six stitches.''

"Well, your grouchiness made it seem like forty." She shifted away to look at the mansion. "Which only proves my point.''

"I have a perfectly fine bedside manner, Miss Baptiste," he said.

"Ha!''

He chuckled, but the sound was more caustic than amused. "I've never had any complaints. You just bring out the grouch in me.''

She eyed him, annoyed. "The knack is mutual, doc. Most people think I'm a lovely person.''

"So you say.'' His grin taunted. "To answer your question, I live here because this is the doctor's cottage. It's closer to the dock and it's where patients have come for fifty years.''

She pondered that, but it didn't wash. "So? That doesn't explain why you live here.''

"Because I'm the doctor, Miss Baptiste.''

She found the remark disturbingly endearing, but squelched the feeling. "What I mean is, you could live in the big house and hike down here for office hours."

He nodded. "I could. But I like living here."

Another ten points for the doctor. He might be a yuppie country sawbones, but he wasn't a pretentious, yuppie country sawbones. She winced. Why was she scoring this guy? It wasn't where he lived on the island that mattered, the point was that he was glued to the island! That was the damning impediment in his character. *Enough woolgathering*!

She stretched her arms over her head, pretending boredom. "Now—if the tour's over, I'd like to get back to my lunch."

His nod was hardly more than a narrowing of the eyes. "We've got a lot to go over this afternoon, Miss Baptiste." He jerked his wrist up to check his watch. "I'd appreciate it if you'd be finished in fifteen minutes."

She ground her teeth. She might owe him, but did he have to be so overbearing? "I thought this was a day off."

"I changed my mind." He placed his palms on the rail and leaned back. "Well? Are you going to eat or not?"

She battled back an urge to push him over

the railing onto the grass. "I'm going," she groused, reminding herself she was there to do his bidding—for *three* endless weeks. "I hope I live through this."

"Did you say something, Miss Baptiste?"

She whirled on him. "The name's Mimi, doc. *Mimi*. It's not that hard. Just two letters, an M and an I. It should be *easy* for you to remember. Just think of yourself, then think of yourself, again! *Me*! *Me*! Get it?" Her sigh was so full of overtones it was almost a curse.

One dark brow rose. "And my name is Marc," he said softly, though she detected an edge to his tone. "Not doc, or sawbones..." his straight glance was accusing "...or sorehead."

She stiffened, momentarily abashed. After fidgeting for a second, she opened her mouth, but didn't know what to say. Conceivably, calling him a sorehead was worse than his continually forgetting her first name.

Besides, she didn't want their relationship to be chummy, so what was her problem with the fact that he called her Miss Baptiste? None at all. It was the best way to deal with him. "On second thought," she mumbled, "call me Miss Baptiste. It's safer."

"Safer?" he repeated, looking skeptical.

She flinched. "For you!" She scrambled for some plausible reason *besides* the truth. "I'll—uh—call you Doctor Merit and you call me Miss Baptiste. That way I won't be as likely to slip up and call you a sorehead in front of your patients." Whew! That was close. She was sure she'd covered her faux pas with glib panache.

Sparking displeasure invaded his glare. "That's very giving of you, Miss Baptiste." He looked at his watch again, a wordless command for her to get moving.

"Okay, I'm going—*sorehead*." As she spun to go, she flicked him a saucy grin. "Let's call that 'one for the road.' Okay?"

"That's *Doctor* Sorehead," he countered.

Annoyance hovered in his eyes, but his lips curved up briefly. Or did they? The impression of amusement was so fleeting Mimi wasn't sure she hadn't merely wished it.

CHAPTER FOUR

By four o'clock Marc had familiarized Mimi with his office and how it ran. He surprised her when he said that next on the agenda was a walk around the island. "Do you have any walking shoes, Miss Baptiste?" he asked.

She hadn't bothered with shoes when she'd gotten dressed. She was perfectly comfortable going barefoot. Glancing down at her feet she wiggled her toes. "Of course, I do, but—"

"Put them on."

She shot him a peevish look. "Honey just *drips* off your tongue, Doc. Asking sweetly the way you did, how can I refuse?" She spun away, muttering something in Bantu that would have made the most worldly Tanzanian blush.

"I didn't quite get that, Miss Baptiste," he called.

"Be grateful for small favors, *Doctor* Merit."

After Mimi put on her battered hiking

boots, they set out across the grassy country-side. Foo Foo scampered along, periodically barking and chasing butterflies. Mimi watched the dog as they walked, since her attention wasn't distracted by any undue chattiness on the doctor's part.

She cast her glowering companion a surreptitious glance every so often as they traversed the mansion's manicured lawn. Against her will she scanned the sharply cut planes of his face. She sensed an inherent strength in the cut of his jaw, as well as a dollop of pigheadedness in the set of his chin.

He had a nice mouth, firm and sensual. *Sensual*? She pinched herself on the arm. *Do not use words like* sensual *when you're thinking about this man, Mimi*, she cautioned. *His mouth is okay as mouths go. Just okay! Think about something else*!

Foo Foo barked at a grasshopper, and Mimi blessed the little varmint for attracting her attention away from Dr. Sensual Mouth. She cleared her throat, determined to get on a different track. ''You know, Doc, I think it's hilarious that a big, surly sawbon—er—man of healing—like yourself would have such a fluffy pet. I'd think you'd gravitate toward those brawny dogs that wear barrels of brandy around their necks. Or a wolf, or even a fluff-ball-eating dingo named Psycho.''

He glanced her way, his expression unamused. ''What, no saber-tooth tiger named Testy?''

She feigned deep concentration, as though the idea had value. ''I'd forgotten about wildcats.'' She nodded. ''Yes, I can see you with a tiger or lion. Even a couple of cranky Persians works for me.'' She thrust her hands in her back pockets. ''So why the Foofer?''

''Foof was left to me by a patient, Anita Landsbury.''

The revelation startled Mimi. ''Left? Like in a will?''

''Not exactly. Anita had no family, and shortly before she passed away she asked me to take care of Foo Foo.'' He gave Mimi a brief look. ''I said I would.''

Mimi pondered his remark for a few seconds, then shrugged. ''You could have found the little mutt a home. Taking care of it didn't mean you had to tie yourself down to it.''

Marc looked at her with something like pity in his eyes. The expression unsettled her. ''It did to me, Miss Baptiste.'' Glancing away, he added, ''You've never had a pet?''

''Sure. Of course, I have.'' That was almost

true. Some lifestyles didn't work well with excess baggage.

He indicated a wooded area. "It's quicker if we cut through this way." His glance was leery. "I'm surprised you had a pet. You don't seem to like animals."

"I love animals! I'm an activist, for Pete's sake! I'm *rabid* on the subject of animals." she retorted, wondering why she allowed him to make her defensive. "It's just that traveling makes it hard to keep a pet, that's all."

"So you like them, you just don't have much to do with them, one to one."

She scowled at him. "What's that supposed to mean?"

He shook his head. "Nothing. Not a thing." With a curious glance he asked, "So, what was this pet you once had?"

Still annoyed by whatever snide point he thought he was making, she muttered, "A bat."

They headed into a woodland of pine and oak trees. Mimi inhaled the rich pungency and felt more at ease. She loved walking through a forest, listening to the birds, the wind. She treasured the restful solitude.

"What kind of cat?" he asked, breaking through her thoughts.

She eyed him askance and couldn't resist a contrary smirk at his mistake. "Vampire."

He cut her a sharp look, and she couldn't help laughing. "I said, *bat*, doc."

"You had a bat for a pet?"

His look of disbelief was classic. Classic and cute. Those sexy brown eyes had gone wide. Dr. Traditional with the fluffy canine apparently hadn't known many women with pet bats.

She lifted a shoulder in a shrug. "It was more like this baby bat fell off the wall of a cave. It would have died, so my dad brought it to camp and we fed it until it could fend for itself."

Marc stopped walking and faced her. "That's a heartwarming story, Miss Baptiste. Thanks for sharing."

His sarcasm made her bristle. "Look, it's perfectly clear we don't see eye-to-eye on things. You like living in one spot. Everybody within who-knows-how-many square miles depends on you. I bet you don't even think about taking vacations because you'd be afraid you'd be gone when you're needed."

Warming to her subject, she poked at his chest. "I've never lived anyplace longer than a few months. The whole world is my home, doc. I'm a traveler, a seeker, like my folks. I want to see everything, experience as much of the world as I can. There's nothing I have that I can't leave behind.'' She held up her braceleted arm. ''Except these charms—and a picture I have of my folks and me. *So what* if I never had a real pet? I've had experiences you'll never have. Never understand. You're the way you are and I'm the way I am.'' She poked again. ''You're a hostage to this island and I have itchy feet. Let's agree to disagree and get along as tolerably as we can for the three weeks I'm here. Okay?'' She poked once more for emphasis, trying not to give too much notice to his solid warmth.

His gaze slid to her poking finger then back to her face. ''I have a salve that will cure that,'' he said, his voice tight.

She frowned, confused. ''Cure what?''

''Itchy feet.'' Pivoting away, he headed down the trail. ''Coming, Miss Baptiste?''

''I don't want my itch cured!'' she shouted. ''Didn't you hear a word I said?''

''I heard you,'' he muttered. ''I just don't give a damn.''

She felt as though she'd been backhanded. ''Oh? Well—that's fine with me!'' Why his indifference hurt was a mystery to her. Still, it stung. Possibly the fact that her parents had been well-known, revered in some circles, had affected her formative years.

She'd received a lot of attention as a girl, growing up in the wilderness with wildlife photographers as world-renowned as André and Renata Baptiste. Doctor Merit's coolness was insulting. Mimi wasn't accustomed to being belittled or snubbed. Her life choices were every bit as worthy as his. She worked for the Earth's endangered creatures and plants. All the money her parents had left her and anything she earned at odd jobs, over and above what she needed for travel and living expenses, went for good causes. *How dare this cantankerous pill pusher not give a damn!*

"This way." He veered right and headed down a steep incline. "Employee housing is beyond the trees. Most of the men are on the mainland until tonight. A few stay on the island, but the married men and most of the rest spend their weekends in Portland. We'll be treating some bloodied faces and plenty of hangovers starting around midnight."

"Yes, Doctor Merit," she said, trying to sound as detached as he did. "Whatever you say, Doctor Merit."

He passed her a grim look. "I'm glad to see your attitude is improving."

Improving! She closed her eyes, exasperated. Either the doctor didn't recognize mockery when he heard it or he had a twisted sense of humor.

Drat the man! He wasn't going to get away with being such a superior smart-aleck! She'd show him. Glaring at his broad back, she started down the slope. "Say, doc, I bet you've never encountered what I think is one of the most overwhelming experiences in the wo—*oooo!*" A loose pebble shot Mimi's boot out from under her. Her backside hit the ground and she launched into a jolting slide.

She cried out, grabbing frantically for purchase. *Anything!* She wasn't picky. A jutting rock, a prominent root. Even a skunk's tail, if the stinker had a good grip on the path. Another few feet and her rear end would be raw meat.

She touched something solid and instinctively grabbed with every appendage she had. Unfortunately, when she threw her legs up and around the object, she dislodged whatever she'd captured, and it, too, gave way. She screamed as she started to slip again, but only for a second before something fell on top of her, terminating her descent. When her scream died in her deflated lungs, she heard a low curse not far away.

Taking a quick mental inventory of her body parts, she decided she'd survived miraculously unscathed—except for some bruising to her posterior. Belatedly, she opened her eyes. Though she'd already begun to get a sneaky inkling, her eyesight confirmed that what had fallen on her was not a tree, as she'd profoundly hoped, but a highly disgruntled doctor. She knew he was disgruntled because his face was too close to hers for her to make any mistake about that. She winced. "Uh— was that you I grabbed?" she asked, her voice weak and raspy.

He looked at her, as though he'd never heard such a stupid question in his life. "Did you have some problem with my hand, Miss Baptiste?" he asked.

"What hand?"

He shifted slightly, to unearth an arm that had been pinned between them and flexed his fingers. "It was exactly like this one, but on the other side. I was holding it out for you to take."

"Oh." She swallowed, ridiculously aware of the heat of his body on hers. "I—I think my eyes were closed.'' In self-defense she blurted, ''But you weren't braced or you wouldn't have fallen when I grabbed your leg!''

His jaws clenched and unclenched. He was so good-looking that even as irritated as he was she reacted strongly to him. ''I was braced, blast it! I just didn't expect you to pry loose my supporting leg.''

She heard a wayward titter and realized it had come from her own throat. The fact that he continued to lounge on top of her, like some Norse god whose job it was to torment mortal females, was obviously getting to her, making her hysterical.

A dark brow arched. ''You think this is funny?''

She shook her head and tried desperately to purse her lips, but another disobedient giggle broke free.

He frowned, but the expression was not as hostile as it was anguished. ''Are you all right?''

She nodded. ''Except for my-uh...'' her face went hot and she couldn't go on. Her heart thudded erratically. Compelling brown eyes made her senses leap to life, and that wasn't good. She didn't want her senses frolicking around a man shackled to an island. She didn't want her emotions laboring under the delusion that he meant anything to her. He didn't! *Couldn't!* With effort, she cleared her throat, feigning an indifference she didn't feel. ''Doc—er—you're lying on me.''

Apparently he hadn't missed that fact, either, since his expression remained troubled. ''I know,'' he whispered hoarsely.

She felt a lurch in her chest. The implication of his quietly spoken words sent an electrical charge through her, a tingling feminine awareness of his intent. Before she could react or even decide how she wanted to react, she heard him groan. His mouth covered hers, hungry and hard, urgent and delicious. His lips were persuasive, moist and firm, demanding a response. Shocked by her own eagerness, she returned his kiss with equal passion.

Coaxing lips parted hers in a soul-stirring message that made her light-headed. Her thoughts spun, her emotions whirled and danced as his kiss held her captive, his thrusting tongue giving birth to a new hunger.

Mimi tasted more than wild passion in his kiss. She also detected impetuous shadings of anger. Anger! She experienced a chilling shock at the realization. He didn't want this any more than she did! Still, something in them, something they couldn't control, excited the other, making them casualties of their own desires.

He wasn't right for her and she wasn't right for him. They both knew that as well as they knew the sun would rise each morning. Yet something in their chemistry drew them, pulled them, compelled them into each other's arms. She had feared and fought this moment from the instant she'd discovered he was a doctor. But she was helpless and so was he. They were pawns, victims of their physical passions and needs.

No! she cried inwardly. *Mimi Baptiste, you are not a victim! You are mistress of your destiny. You are a woman without strings, and you know in your heart this man would bind you, body and soul, and you could never break free! Do you want to leave your heart on this island when you go? Because, you will go. You must go! Save your love for a man like your father. A man who craves adventure, is restless for fresh horizons. Save yourself, Mimi, before it's too late!*

She heard a whimper from deep in her throat as some small kernel of sanity survived inside her. That tiny spark of reason fought his allure, desperate to resist the deep, achingly seductive exploration of her mouth. With the greatest reluctance she'd ever experienced, she dredged up the grit to press against his chest and turned her face away. "Stop it," she cried, her words hardly more than a rush of air. "Get off me!" Her arms trembled with the struggle to push him away. Though wobbly of body and mind, she persisted in her attempt to break free, defying his magnetism with her last dregs of strength.

As suddenly as the kiss had begun, it ended. Marc rolled away and sat up. Mimi wasn't sure, but she thought she heard a guttural growl. Was he angry with her or himself? She blinked, staring at him. His back to her, he dragged both hands through his hair. For a moment he dipped his head, as though attempting to regain control.

Mimi felt something cold on her cheek and shifted to find Foo Foo sniffing her. She winced and pushed up to her elbows. "I'm not dead," she grumbled. "Keep your cold nose out of my face."

"Yeah, I'll remember that," Marc muttered. Pushing up, he turned to face her, his expression stony.

She flicked him a wary glance. "I was talking to—"

"I know." His jaw shifted from left to right and his nostrils flared. He extended a hand. "The least I can do is help you up."

She swallowed, hesitating. Her lips still throbbed from his kiss. She wasn't sure she dared his touch quite so soon after....

Shaking her head, she planted her hands on the ground and shoved herself up to an unsteady stance. Reluctant to meet his eyes, she allowed her gaze to trail after Foo Foo as the fuzz-ball headed down the trail, tail wagging as though nothing earth-shattering had just happened. Inhaling for strength, Mimi struck out to follow the dog.

"Do you need any help...?"

"Don't touch me!" She sidestepped away, coming to a stumbling halt. Refusing to look at him, she pointedly stuffed her hands in her hip pockets. "Just lead."

The scuff of boot leather told her he'd begun to trudge forward, but a second later, he came to a halt beside her. "I'm sorry," he said. "That was stupid and—"

"I agree," she cut in. "Forget it. Let's talk about something else."

He didn't move for several heartbeats, and

she wondered if he was looking at her. She couldn't allow herself to glance his way. She might burst into tears. Biting her lip to keep it from trembling she watched Foo Foo prance toward the distant clearing. With a jerky nod she indicated the direction. "Just go."

He moved into her line of vision and she swallowed around a painful lump. As her senses returned, she felt a heaviness in her chest, and a sickening sensation of emptiness, a hollowness she'd never experienced before.

With a rush of bitter anger, she squelched the feeling. How ridiculous. Talk about letting her imagination run away with her. Obviously she was still feeling the insidious effects of Marc's kiss. Her hormones were just surging or something. She wasn't empty or lonely. She had a great life, teeming with adventure and good deeds.

Straightening her shoulders, she struck out after him. She was no man's love slave! She wouldn't let one impulsive act disrupt her life. Determined to get herself on a less dangerous track she cast around in her mind for something to distract her from—well, to distract her. Luckily, the path had leveled off and they were only about twenty feet from bright sunlight.

"What were we talking about?" she asked, her voice raspy.

He half turned, then seemed to think better of it. "Hell if I know."

She flinched at his gruff tone. "You don't have to bite my head off. I didn't kiss *you*, you know!"

His head snapped up as though he hadn't expected her to belt him between the eyes with it. Abruptly, he pivoted to face her, blocking her path. His mouth was set in annoyance, his accusing gaze riveted on her. "You—" He cut himself off and ground his teeth. "You—" His glance shot away then back, his mouth working. She didn't know what he had in mind to say, but he didn't seem to be able to find the right words. She certainly hoped it didn't have anything to do with the possibility that she did a little kissing back! That had nothing to do with the fact that he started it, and that made it *his* fault!

Finally with a low groan he shook his head. "To hell with it." He started to turn away, then stopped, his expression troubled. Mini sensed the supercharged tension between them and shifted uneasily. They were both cross, both weighted down by guilt and anxiety over their loss of control, but she could see that Marc was battling to discipline himself.

"I think," he said, at last, all gruffness gone from his voice, "that you were telling me about an overwhelming experience." He crossed his arms loosely, suddenly all smooth indifference. "So, Miss Baptiste, what is so overwhelming to you that you felt like sharing?"

She experienced an absurd rush of tears, and blinked them back. In an ironic twist of fate, her most overwhelming experience had just become the kiss of a certain painfully inappropriate doctor. It was eerie how something that had, only moments ago, seemed significant could be erased in the blink of an eye or the slip of a boot.

She gulped hard in an attempt to get herself under control. "Oh..." she nodded. "I remember. I—I was saying I bet you'd never encountered what I thought—*think* is one of the most overwhelming experiences in the world."

She sniffed and rubbed a shaky hand across an eye, hoping it looked more like she was brushing away a hair or bit of grass than a tear. "Right. I—it was...it's walking through the forest...." She was grateful that she sounded calm because she ached inside. This little speech was no longer true, but she forged on. "Walking in the vast silence, then hearing an elk bugle in the distance. It's the most extraordinary primeval experience you can imagine." She sucked in a tremulous breath, forcing herself to meet his gaze.

Slowly a glittering mockery invaded his stare. "No, it isn't, Miss Baptiste."

He had turned his back and trekked into the light before Mimi absorbed his suggestive implication.

CHAPTER FIVE

MARC couldn't believe what he had done in the woods that afternoon. He'd actually *kissed* Mimi Baptiste! On second thought, *kissed* was too tame a word for what had taken place in that shadowy glade. After all the lecturing he'd done to himself on the dangers of becoming involved with a globe-trotting imp, he had kissed her. The act may have been unpremeditated, but it didn't make his rashness less appalling. *What had possessed him?*

He winced at the stupidity of the question. He knew exactly what had possessed him. A pair of silvery eyes. Lips that taunted with artful smiles that torqued his gut into knots. Not to mention her spirit and sass. All those things drew him, tempted him. Then, suddenly, he'd been thrown on top of her, the sweet softness of her body pressed against him. And he'd lost it. That's all he could think. He'd just lost it.

For years, he'd been too busy to have a social life. He still was, for that matter. He couldn't count the number of times doctor buddies had told him he was ridiculously picky when it came to women. "Just go have some fun," they'd say. But he rarely did.

So the fuse to his libido was doubtless already sizzling, ready to explode. He'd fended off his nurse, Ursula, for weeks. That probably had something to do with his reckless behavior, too. Unfortunately for Mimi, she'd been in the wrong place at the wrong time.

Yeah, sure, he grumbled inwardly. *And she just had the wrong eyes and the wrong lips.* He flinched. *Face it, Merit. You're hot for this woman and if you don't get a grip on yourself you're going to do something you'll really regret.*

How badly might falling for such a flitting butterfly affect him? He already had a clue. Even now, recalling their kiss gave him fits, sending hot spikes of desire though him. Her tang lingered on his lips and preyed on his mind. She tasted like fresh air after rain, or the way a summer night on an African savanna might smell—clean, warm and lush.

"Marc!"

He heard his name and fell to earth with a crash. Glancing around, he realized everybody was staring at him. The last thing he remembered, he'd been enjoying a pleasant family dinner on the mansion's loggia, welcoming the light scent from the rose gardens. He'd also taken a certain guilty pleasure in scanning Mimi's animated face as she sat across the table in his direct line of vision. All through dinner she'd ignored him with a vengeance, though she'd chatted amiably with Jake, George and Susan, and admired Kyle, now propped in his mommy's lap, happily gurgling and wagging his pudgy arms.

From the look of everyone's plates, it was obvious dinner was over. Good Lord, he'd actually drifted off. *Get into the game, Merit!* "What?" he asked nobody in particular.

The man to his left, at the head of the table, laughed. "What's the matter with you, little brother? Losing your hearing?"

Marc faced Jake, his expression as casual as he could make it, considering his absurd mental meanderings. "I'm sorry, I was thinking about—a case," he lied, then leaned forward, giving his brother his full attention. "What did you say?"

"I said, I understand you're kidnapping your assistants these days." He winked at Mimi and Marc noticed that her answering smile was stunning, nothing like anything she'd ever flashed his way. "From the evidence on her head, I'd say you've gotten into violence, too." Jake placed his forearms on the table's surface of green Portuguese tiles. "I don't applaud your methods, but allow me to compliment your taste."

Mimi laughed. "Why, thank you, Jake." She beamed at him. "I'm glad to know not *all* of the Merit men are bullying women snatchers." She eyed Marc briefly in the same high dudgeon as she had displayed ever since the kiss, then flicked her attention back to Jake. "But meeting you and Susan, George and the baby have made up for my—bad luck." This time her glance was so brief Marc would have believed he'd only imagined it, except for its sting.

He sat back in his chair, the creak of wicker a subtle criticism of its own, and crossed his arms over his chest. "Believe me, Jake," he said, forcing his glance to his brother, "I'm paying for my pillage. I've rarely met a more exasperating, mouthy female." When their glances clashed, Mimi's affronted scowl made him grin. "Which only proves the old axiom, 'crime doesn't pay.'"

Susan giggled and lifted Kyle to her shoulder, patting his back. "This is all very entertaining, boys and girls, but my son needs some attention in the diapering department." A scraping sound drew Marc's attention to Jake as he stood. "I'll do it, darling." He lifted the infant from his wife's arms. "You stay and talk." He bent and kissed her lovingly on the lips.

"Bring Kyle back and we'll put him in the playpen while we visit," she whispered, her freckled cheeks flushing a bright red.

"Good idea."

As Susan readjusted her napkin and her composure, Marc moved his attention unwillingly to Mimi. She glanced toward the foot of the table where George sat, clad in a crimson velvet smoking jacket. The unsmiling elder Merit was engrossed in watching Jake carry away his grandson. Old King George, as his sons often referred to him, carried himself with a regal bearing. Marc had to admit, with his father's sharp, patrician features and that silver mane of hair, he was the image of an austere potentate.

As far back as Marc could remember, friends and enemies alike had commented that the Merit sons had inherited their father's good looks and their mother's friendly nature. Marc chuckled darkly, covering it with a cough. Except for Mimi Baptiste! She couldn't be convinced that Marc had a friendly bone in his body.

As he examined his father, he was struck by the softening he'd seen in his stern, over-bearing nature since Kyle had come into their lives, a newborn, four months ago. The old man still had his tyrannical moments, but the baby was such a joy to him, he was *almost* a pleasure to be around. But not quite.

"George," Mimi said, "Susan tells me you play chess."

The elder Merit's attention flew to their guest. "I do." He squinted at her. "Why? Do you enjoy the game?"

Mimi grinned. "I'm a chess nut. My dad and I used to play for hours in the evenings by lantern light." She made a self-conscious face that Marc found engaging. "I'm never going to be a great chess player, but if you enjoy chess, I'd love to play."

"If he *enjoys*..." Both Susan and Marc started that sentence together. Glancing at each other, they burst out laughing. Marc went on, "Miss Baptiste, my father doesn't *enjoy* chess, he lives and breathes the game. If you agree to play with him, you'd better have the guts of a kamikaze pilot, the conviction of a zealot and the agility of a Wimbledon tennis champ.'' He watched her, his crooked grin challenging. ''And you'd better be good, because if you're not, he'll eat you alive.''

Mimi turned to Susan. ''Agility?'' she asked.

Susan laughed. ''He tends to throw chess pieces.''

''Lies, vile lies!'' George interrupted, reaching out to touch Mimi's hand. ''Don't let these rapscallions dissuade you, dear girl.'' He patted her hand. ''I'm merely a chess enthusiast hoping another enthusiast will agree to spend a little time after dinner indulging in a mutually enjoyable pastime.'' He lifted his chin to glare at Marc. ''And you—stop pestering her. You've done her enough damage.'' He patted Mimi's hand again. ''Poor child, with your stitched-up wound.''

Marc shook his head at his father's manipulation. ''Enter my father's chess lair at your own risk, Miss Baptiste.''

''And wear a hard hat,'' Susan added, earning for herself a severe look from her father-in-law. She giggled. ''Okay, okay, George.'' She held up her hands in surrender. ''I won't say another word.''

''Another word about what?'' Jake asked as

he returned to the covered verandah with Kyle.

"About your father and his notorious behavior when it comes to the game of chess."

Jake leaned over to place Kyle in the playpen, set up amid the droves of antique wicker chaises, chairs, tables and potted plants that made up the seating areas in the sheltered loggia. As he began to straighten, he paused and glanced at them, his expression dubious. "Lord, no. King George hasn't tried to con Mimi into playing?" Jake looked at the blond newcomer. "You haven't *offered* to play, I hope?"

Mimi scanned their faces then tossed them an impertinent grin so dazzling it sent a prickle of restlessness along Marc's spine. Rising to her feet, she took George's hand, her move accompanied by the tinkle of silver charms. "Come on, Georgie," she coaxed. "Let's ditch these party poopers and go have some fun."

The elder Merit stood and with theatrical chivalry offered Mimi his arm. "If you peons will excuse us, Mademoiselle Baptiste and I shall take our leave." He placed his hand over the one she'd put on his forearm, and turned away, leading Mimi into the mansion. He said something to her and she laughed. The light sound ricocheted around in Marc's head long after the door to the loggia closed.

"Marc!"

He jerked back to consciousness, irritated that his mind seemed bent on trailing after Mimi Baptiste like that of a schoolboy tormented by his first crush. He cleared his throat and got his bearings. Susan stood beside his chair, looking concerned. Jake sat on one of the cushioned wicker chaises. Lounging back, he looked at his younger brother as though he'd never seen him before.

"What's wrong with you tonight?" Jake asked, his expression calculating. "Does your trance-like state have anything to do with 'Miss Baptiste'?" His emphasis on her surname was telling. Jake detected a subtext to Marc's seemingly insignificant association with the blonde, and he wasn't buying the 'insignificant' part. Blast his brother and his intuitive nature.

"No, it doesn't have anything to do with Miss Baptiste," he said, too vehemently.

Susan held out a hand. "Come on over and join the family." When he didn't immediately take her up on her offer, she grasped his hand

and tugged. "We get a good long visit so rarely, Marc. Come sit down."

At Susan's coaxing, he stood, deciding lingering at the table was silly. After all, he had the chance to visit his brother and sister-in-law too infrequently as it was. Allowing some trivial, momentary infatuation to annoy him so much that he couldn't enjoy his time with them was a foolish waste.

As he passed the playpen, he knelt to view his nephew. Lying on his back, Kyle happily examined a foot as though it were one of the wonders of the world. The infant was chubby and pink. He wore a halo of wispy blond hair and his eyes were a dark blue that Marc sensed would one day be a deep, rich brown. Kyle was a precious cherub with cherubic cheeks and a valentine for a mouth. The sight touched something inside of him, a need so strong he'd left a successful practice in Boston to come back to Merit Island. He'd hoped to find a woman from the area to share his life with, someone who appreciated simple, quiet living, who wanted children, and who valued a sense of belonging and being needed. Just because he hadn't found her yet didn't mean he wouldn't.

Kyle stuck a toe in his mouth and Marc

found himself smiling. "Cute kid," he murmured.

A light hand on his shoulder told him Susan had lingered to gaze at her child, too. "A dream come true." She brushed his temple with a kiss. "Come on. Sit. Let's talk while Kyle is being a good boy." Marc looked up at his attractive sister-in-law as she smiled. "I'd say we have about fifteen minutes before little Mr. Aren't-My-Toes-Delicious realizes there isn't much nourishment in his digits and demands food."

Marc took a seat on a wicker couch cushioned in white cotton with a fern design. The low coffee table that separated him from Jake had a tile top perfect for propping feet. He promptly settled his boots on the green surface. "Nice night," he said, lounging both arms along the length of the sofa back.

Susan curled up beside Jake on the broad chaise, snuggling beneath his arm. Jake's curious squint remained on his brother. "You never answered my question."

Marc remembered the question but passed his brother a "don't go there" look and laid his head back to stare up at the ceiling. "Long week," he muttered, determined to change the subject.

"So—why do you call her Miss Baptiste?" Susan asked.

He flinched at the continued badgering and eyed them grudgingly. Jake's grin was shrewd. Susan looked curious.

"Shut up, big brother!" he grumbled.

Jake laughed. "Good lord. Hook, line and sinker! Who would have thought!"

Susan peered first at her chuckling husband, then at Marc, then back at Jake. "Are you two communicating in some kind of psychic brotherly telepathy? I'm lost."

"Marc's gone and fallen in love," Jake said.

Though the remark was made in an aside that was little more than a whisper, Marc heard it like the thunder of a cannon, and leapt to his feet. "*You're nuts!*" He was furious that Jake would even *think* anything so ludicrous, let alone say it out loud.

Jake canted his head to grin at his brother, not appearing terribly distressed that Marc had just maligned his mental state. "You're in love with Mimi Baptiste, and you don't want to be. Right?"

He ground his teeth. "I'm not in love with her, but you're right about one thing. I certainly don't want to be!"

"Why not?" Susan interjected. "I think she's darling."

"Darling?" Marc repeated, his tone scornful. "The woman is a gypsy! She thinks living in one place is tantamount to a sin and anybody who would dare such a transgression is cursed. Jake's just a *little* nuts when compared to Mimi. If nuttiness had a country she'd be its queen!"

Susan's puzzled expression softened into a smile. "My, my. Such passion from our cool, collected physician." She turned to gaze up at her husband. "You know what, honey?" she asked, "I think you're right. I think Marc is infatuated with an original character, and it goes against his grain." She faced her brother-in-law. "Poor Marc. He wanted Miss Pipe-and-Slippers and he got Miss Piping-Hot!"

"I did not got—er—I did not get her. I don't want her! Is that abundantly clear?"

"Yeah," Jake said, raising a mocking brow. "I'm clear. Are you clear, Susan?"

"Oh—absolutely." She nodded, but continued to smile at Marc. "You don't want her. Which is exactly the way you felt about Ursula, if I remember correctly."

"Right," Marc said, though he detected a *but*.

."But you called your nurse Ursula."

A wave of gray passed before Marc's eyes, like a dark premonition. *No*! he told whatever it was that was trying to violate his consciousness. *I won't listen*! "I feel absolutely no attraction for Mimi Baptiste," he bit out, bent on convincing himself of that fact. "The idea is so demented, it's laughable. Any woman I might one day fall in love with would have to be one hundred percent stable, and Mimi is as stable as—as nitroglycerin."

"Nitro, huh?"

Marc slashed a troubled glance toward the double doors that led out to the loggia, unhappy to see Mimi standing there. All sound seemed to cease. Even the breeze stopped blowing and sea birds froze in mid-shriek.

Golden light from lantern-style wall sconces illuminated her expression, which Marc could only describe as damning. After a tense second, she broke eye contact with him and headed onto the stone patio, gesturing toward the dining table. "George forgot his glasses." Scooping them up she pivoted around, then came to a halt, stabbing Marc with a lethal glare. "Just for the record, Doctor Merit, I wouldn't have a stodgy, needle-happy fusspot like you if you were served up to me over rice with drawn butter and lemon juice!''

She shifted toward Susan and Jake. ''Thanks for the dinner,'' she said, clearly disciplining her voice. ''It was lovely...'' She eyed Marc fleetingly. ''For the most part.''

When she was gone, Jake's low laugh rumbled through the dusky quiet.

Marc scowled at his brother. ''What's so blasted hilarious?''

Jake hugged Susan close. ''It looks like we've found the legendary irresistible force and immovable object—namely Mimi and Marc. Or should I say the firebrand and the fusspot?''

''That's very cute,'' Marc retorted. ''Maybe you should take your comedy act to Vegas. *Now*.''

With a casual sweep of an arm, Jake indicated the door through which the blonde had disappeared. ''Whatever you've done to her, you've done with shrewd finesse. She's downright wild about you.'' His lips twitched with wry humor. ''These next three weeks should be entertaining.''

''Yeah,'' Marc groused, ''like the flu.'' Turning on his heel, he plunged his hands in his jeans pockets and headed for the lawn. ''If it's not overly chaotic to Miss Baptiste's social schedule, tell her to set her alarm for five.''

"Yep," Jake called. "*Very* entertaining.''

Mimi's first day as Marc's assistant had been long, brutal and enlightening. Between a broken finger and pinkeye, she'd discovered this aquatic hunk of real estate was called Merit Island, something the doctor had neglected to tell her. Not long after that, another patient had mentioned the ''mine,'' revealing it was for *emeralds*, of all things!

Apparently Marc Merit was worth a fortune. Another detail he'd neither mentioned nor seemed particularly concerned with. Mimi had never met a multi-zillionaire before, so discovering the doctor was one took her by surprise. She wondered why he even worked, let alone at such a stressful, unrelenting profession.

She was starving and exhausted, but dinner had yet to materialize. Marc had showered and changed out of his doctorly beige trousers, white knit shirt and white coat, and now stood at the kitchen counter in jeans and a forest-green turtleneck, the sleeves pushed up to his elbows. With his back turned, he was chopping vegetables and ignoring the pants off her.

She'd been barked orders to brown the chicken that would eventually be combined with vegetables and rice to become a quick, hearty casserole. That couldn't come too soon for her. She'd never worked so hard or so long without food in her life. Starting at midnight last night, they'd nursed cuts and bruises and treated hangovers until two, then they were up at five, throwing down a quick breakfast of coffee and oatmeal before patients started arriving at seven. She hadn't had a break or a bite since. Not until the last patient limped out of the office at seven that evening. Thirty minutes ago.

She shifted to stare at the doctor's profile. He didn't look particularly tired. Of course, he jumped headfirst into his role as healer six days a week, fifty-two weeks a year. *Six days a week, fifty-two weeks a year*? Her mind wouldn't even compute such a grinding, mind-numbing schedule.

Covertly watching her pensive host, she had to admit he seemed to thrive on the work. All day long, he'd had a smile for everybody— but her. If she hadn't witnessed it herself, she would never have guessed he had such a down-home, benevolent grace with people. Everybody loved him. Island employees and folks from surrounding atolls all called him "Doctor Marc" with genuine esteem and affection, as though he were a brother or an uncle or cousin who had become the pride of their family.

The few women who'd come to his office exhibited all that and one more significant sentiment. Calculated interest.

She eyed the tall, good-looking physician as several questions nagged at her to be voiced.

"Say, doc?" she called, deciding she'd had enough of addressing him as Dr. Merit to last her for at least twelve hours. "What was the diagnosis for that last woman this afternoon?"

She watched as his expression closed in thought. He glanced her way briefly. "What woman?"

What woman, she jeered inwardly. Due to a scarcity of females on Merit Island and the surrounding rocks, there had only been three all day. "The one in the acid-yellow sweater and black leather skirt." She tried to keep the leery quality from her voice. "You must remember her—her sore throat."

Nodding, he turned back to his chopping. "Madeline."

She gritted her teeth at his use of her first name. "Whatever. So what did she have?"

He cast her a quick, speculative gaze. "Wouldn't that fall under doctor-patient privilege?"

She shrugged. "Oh?" Dragging her attention back to her chicken tending, she made a face. "I didn't think she looked so sick she needed to come fifteen miles by boat to have you look down her throat. That's all."

He didn't respond, so she peeked at him. "What's the doctor-patient rule about—dating?" She opted for a relatively mild word, considering what she was thinking.

He looked at her. This time his frown was admonishing. "Are you suggesting I am anything less than professional when I'm examining a patient?"

"Don't get huffy, doc. What you do behind that screen is your business. Madeline just looked more like a woman with a case of lust than lockjaw."

His brows nipped in a fraction. She was startled when he laid down his knife and turned. Lounging against the cabinet, he eyed her, his features grim. "Let's get this out in the open, deal with it and not talk about it again, okay?"

Confused and unsettled, she nodded cautiously. What was he going to say? That he and Madeline had a sexual liaison from time to time in his office—to relieve tensions—and just how often and with whom he philandered was none of her business? She swallowed hard, wishing she'd kept her stupid curiosity to herself.

"That thing in the woods between us was a mistake," he said, startling her by the lurching change of subject. "I'd think you'd realize by now that my rashness had more to do with the fact that I *don't* dally with my patients than it had to do with you." He slid his gaze away, and she could tell he was struggling to keep from snarling at her for making such a lewd suggestion. When his glance found hers again, he seemed calmer, but unhappy. "Once and for all, I apologize. It wasn't the norm for me, and I would give anything to take it back."

She blinked, oddly annoyed. She supposed he was making it clear that no matter what had prompted Madeline to come to him, the only contact between them had been professional. Still, his need to condemn the kiss to prove he wasn't a letch wounded her feminine pride. She couldn't fathom why. Didn't she want to forget it, too? Didn't she also see it as a blunder, sprung from human failing?

Peeved, she slammed down her kitchen fork. "Don't you worry doc, I forgot it the minute it happened!" She planted her fists on her hips. "Now what?"

He looked down at the pine floor then met her gaze. "I suppose we try to get along."

She sniffed contemptuously, not even attempting to reign in her temper. Marc Merit made her anxious and uneasy and she'd had a bellyful today, with his alluring scent, his accidental touches that sang through her veins and his disturbing brown eyes. She was so tense, she wanted to scream. That statement about forgetting his kiss was pure fiction, and she hated herself for holding the memory so foolishly dear. "I *meant* what else do you want me to do for dinner, doc? The chicken's brown."

He pursed his lips, and Mimi sensed the expression denoted aggravation rather than deep thought. He viewed her from beneath half-closed lids. "I don't know the niceties of dining in the jungle, but in our local culture—however mundane and monotonous it may be—we often do what we call 'setting the table,' which consists of placing metal implements called—''

''That's terribly clever,'' she cut in, spinning toward the cabinet where the dishes were kept. ''You're wasted as a doctor. In Las Vegas your comedy act could earn you—oh, with your talent I can't even imagine your worth.'' Grabbing two plates she spun on him. ''Maybe—*coffee*?''

''Funny you should mention Las Vegas,'' he grumbled.

''What?''

With a negating shake of his head he muttered, ''Forget it.'' Turning away, he gathered the chopped vegetables into a bowl, then moved to set it next to the stove. She attempted to reign in her anger, but failed, slamming the plates down. Whirling to get the silverware, she came to a skidding halt. She and Marc were suddenly nose to chest. Mere inches apart. Instinctively, she backed a step away and so did he. They stared at each other for an overlong moment that rang with tension. Finally, Marc indicated a direction. ''I'll get the coffee mugs.''

His emphasis on the word *coffee* didn't escape her. She experienced a triumphant tingle at getting his goat, and flashed an impertinent grin. She had no idea why mustering his passion, however slight, was so earth-shattering in importance. Deciding she didn't want to think about it, she grabbed two handfuls of silverware from a drawer and was all the way back to the table before she realized she wasn't setting places for twelve.

They almost ran into each other again when she returned with the correct amount of silver. This time she managed to react first, and indicated the table with a broad wave. "Be my guest."

He thumped the mugs down near their plates. As she distributed the flatware, she heard sizzling and realized he'd added the vegetables to the chicken. "How did the chess game go last night?" he asked.

Surprised by the question, she pivoted around to glower at his back. "Fine."

He peered at her, his brow creased with doubt.

She made a half shrug. "He won, but tonight I'll get even. I haven't played in a long time."

He turned away from the stove. "Tonight?"

She brushed a strand of hair behind her ear. She'd confined the flyaway stuff in one braid this morning, thinking it would be more appropriate for working in a doctor's office. But now disobedient strands drooped all around her face. It was like trying see through the dangling branches of a weeping willow. She blew upward, launching airy locks out of her eyes. "Do you have any problem with me playing chess with your father tonight?"

"No problem. It's your sleep to lose." He slid his hands into his jeans pockets, the move cruelly sexy. "You must really like chess."

"I do." She lifted her chin. "Why shouldn't I?"

He made a nonchalant gesture. "No reason." His gaze lingered for another palpable moment before he turned away to stir the food. "You said it's been a long time since you played chess?"

"Not since my parents—" The word still stuck in her throat. "Died," she whispered at last.

He didn't respond for a long time. Merely stood, stirring the food.

"If you don't mind my asking," he said at last, "How did your parents die?"

Though she'd brought up the subject, his inquiry hit like a boot in the belly, and she sank to one of the kitchen chairs. The memory of that horrible day was still vivid and raw in her memory. "In a flood." She rested her elbows on the table and laid her head in her hands. After a sigh, she added, "We were crossing a river in Kenya. There'd been flooding in the mountains, but we didn't know it. Suddenly, as we waded across, a great wall of water came crashing down on us from upstream. I was nearest to shore, so I made it." She stopped, the jarring memory stealing her ability to speak. After a deep, restorative breath, she whispered, "They—" Her voice broke and she had to swallow several times to regain herself. "That was ten years ago."

"How old were you?" he asked softly.

"Seventeen."

He said nothing for a long time. Finally, he murmured, "I'm sorry."

She sensed compassion in his tone and angled her head to look at him. "Thanks." she murmured. "Me, too."

He stood there, on the plus side of six feet, slim but powerfully built. Dr. Body Perfect, dressed in jeans and his signature slouch. Oddly, she had a feeling his frown was due less to his displeasure at her than to some kind of internal conflict.

The kitchen clock's tick could barely be

heard over the sizzle of vegetables and meat. She began to count each beat, since the other option was to run screaming into the sea. She hadn't taken the kiss at all well. Ever since it had happened, she'd been snapping and gnashing her teeth at him like some wounded, wild animal. Why this man had the ability to drive her wacky was beyond her. And why he had the capacity to capture her gaze and hold it was troubling, even frightening.

"Look, Miss Baptiste," he said at last, his expression serious and somehow determined. "I've changed my mind. I'll pay for the damage to your friend's catamaran. I'll pay for you to go wherever you want." He straightened, slipping his hands back into his pockets. "You can leave tomorrow."

CHAPTER SIX

Mimi was so shocked she couldn't speak, couldn't even absorb his offer. After a minute, she sat back, staring. "You—you want me to leave—tomorrow?"

He lifted his chin in a half nod.

An odd volatile feeling invaded her stomach. She'd never experienced it before and didn't know what to make of it—excitement or indignation. "Why? Didn't I do a good job today? Did you hire somebody else?"

He shook his head, his gaze lifting to somewhere above her. "You did fine. I just think it would be better if you go."

She frowned at him, wondering at her hesitancy to leap into the air and click her heels with joy. Wasn't it her fondest wish to be released from her three-week imprisonment with this disturbing stick-in-the-mud with the sexy eyes and gentle touch?

Well, wasn't it?

She dropped her gaze to her lap and fumbled with her belt buckle, trying to understand her hesitation. Why did she feel like an unsatisfactory hireling sent packing? *Why wasn't she packing?* She peered up at him. "I worked like an ox, today, doc," she murmured.

He returned his gaze to hers but didn't speak.

"You can't keep up this pace alone for three weeks, and you know it." What was she doing? Why was she arguing *against* leaving?

He pressed his lips together in obvious irritation. Still, he didn't respond.

Anger surged through her and she vaulted up to stand. "Look, doc," she began, with absolutely no idea what she planned to say, but knowing something had to be said whether she wanted to say it or not. "I realize we get on each other's nerves, and I gather you have the money to pay for the repairs, but I'm *insulted* that you'd think I would merrily accept your blasted charity and walk away." She stalked over to him and poked his chest. "I don't hit men, but consider your face slapped." She poked again. "I pay my way and don't you forget it." She poked, poked, poked for emphasis. When she started to poke him again, she found her hand caught in his.

"Miss Baptiste," he said, his tone cautionary, "Do that one more time and you'll play chess standing up." His eyes glittered with meaning.

She gasped and stepped back, attempting to tug from his grasp, but he refused to relinquish her hand. "You—I—" she stuttered, struggling to get her mind on track. "*Women* do not sit still for physical abuse these days, Doc." She glowered at him, but inside she fought to ignore the flutter in her chest at his provoking nearness.

"Just so you'll know, Miss Baptiste..." His pause was short, no longer than a breath, but prolonged enough for her nerves to stretch taut and begin to fray. He dipped close and she reacted without benefit of thought. Lifting her chin and closing her eyes, she puckered up. "Neither do men," he whispered, his lips grazing her ear.

He abruptly released her hand and she stumbled backward. When she opened her eyes, he'd turned away.

Mimi's first week as Doctor Merit's assistant had been tiring, but also rewarding in an odd way. She'd never worked so hard in her life, yet she'd begun to get an inkling of why the doctor loved what he did and why he stayed.

All she had to do was witness an old man's teary gratitude when "Doctor Marc" told him his wife of forty-three years was out of danger after a sudden, virulent infection had nearly taken her life the week before.

Mimi also recalled how the young, frightened bride of a fisherman had clasped Marc's hand tightly, crying, making him swear he would be there when her baby decided to be born. He'd smiled at her and cupped her face in his big hand, whispering his promise. The girl's relief had been so evident it had affected Mimi strongly.

She remembered how she'd stared at Marc, struck by the fact that he was a saint to these people. This fearful teenage bride, living on a sparsely populated rock with her fisherman husband, so far from her mainland roots, clung to Marc's promise as though it were a safety line thrown to her as she struggled to keep from drowning in a rough sea.

Mimi had found herself chatting quietly with the young wife over a cup of coffee while Marc instructed her nervous husband on what to do when his wife went into labor until he arrived. Mimi had learned from her parents not to whimper and whine and obsess about things life threw at her—rather to depend on herself and her family to see troubles through. Indicating the boyish husband, Mimi had said, "Give Rafe a chance to be strong for you. Together, you can have this baby by yourselves if you have to."

She related how she'd seen aboriginal woman give birth as though it were an everyday occurrence. "Because it is," she'd added. "Doctor Marc will be here as soon as possible, but trust yourself and your husband." She gave the young man a long, serious look, then smiled encouragingly. "I bet Rafe can handle about anything. Don't you?"

The teen seemed to ponder this, then nodded, the beginnings of a smile curving her lips. "He's very smart," she whispered.

With a squeeze of the girl's hand, Mimi had left, sensing the couple could handle things if the need arose. She'd felt strangely buoyant about her contribution. On the boat trip back to Merit Island, she and Marc had spoken little. However, one thing he did say, did do, stuck in her mind. He'd glanced her way and murmured, "Thanks for the advice you gave Sally. She needs to learn to believe in herself and her husband."

Mimi hadn't realized he'd heard. Not knowing how to respond, she'd nodded and turned away. But even now, days later, she remembered his compliment with disquiet, recollecting how an unanticipated warmth had radiated through her body, making her tingle.

"I refuse to tingle!" she mumbled as she tramped toward a secluded cove behind the cottage. She'd seen the place from her bedroom window and decided that the first chance she got, she'd go swimming. It was late and she was tired. The water would be chilly, but that was fine with her. She'd been thinking too many warm, fuzzy thoughts about a certain— well, somebody she didn't want to think warm, fuzzy thoughts about. She needed cooling off. And she needed to work off some energy. Not that she wasn't pooped, but this energy came from another part of her, an energy that needed to be doused to death.

She heard yapping and twisted around. Foo Foo scampered down the grassy slope after her. She glowered at the puff-ball. "Just where do you think you're going?" She exhaled, exasperated. The mutt seemed to have decided Mimi belonged to her. She couldn't eat without the tiny botheration leaping into her lap. And if she didn't get her bedroom door closed tightly, Foo Foo would barge in and hop on the bed. After the first couple of nights, when she'd hustled the doggie back out, she'd given up and let it snuggle against her back.

Though she hated herself for getting soft about the tiny beast, she couldn't suppress a grin. "I don't want you down there, young lady. I won't be responsible. You're so runty anything might eat you—a turtle, a clam! A guppy! Why aren't you annoying the doc?"

Foo Foo yapped and bounced and wagged, not looking chastised or deterred.

Mimi knew Marc had received a couple of applications for the job and was speaking with the women, doing preliminary interviews by phone. Apparently, Foo Foo found that boring.

Spinning on her heel, she ordered, "Go back to the house, Foofy!" She hadn't gone two steps when a white blur whizzed in front of her, then turned and yapped. She plunked her fists on her hips. "You are a naughty dog! Go home!"

Foo Foo's tail waggled so hard it looked like it might snap off. Her barks were so enthusiastic, her forepaws lifted off the ground.

Mimi eyed the starry night. "Okay. You can come, but you have to sit quietly while I swim."

Foo Foo yapped, and Mimi had grave doubts that the dog's plans included even a smattering of obedience. "Why is it that you do what the doc says, but around me you're the houndlet of the Baskervilles?"

Foo Foo ran in mindless circles, completely engrossed in play. With a laugh, Mimi decided to go about her business and ignore the insubordinate little cur.

A safe distance from the surging surf, she laid her towel on the sand and kicked out of her scuffs. Slipping off her shorts and blouse, she tossed them onto her towel. After a second's hesitation, she doffed her bra and panties and added them to the pile before dashing into the rollers. With a running lunge, she executing a shallow dive. The sensation of chilly ocean water rushing over her bare skin rejuvenated her, and she surfaced with a whoop of joy.

Turning toward shore, she caught a wave and body surfed until her knees hit sand, then she spun around, whooping and diving. After several more times, she felt her tension falling away in great sheets. Not until now had she realized how much strain she'd been under since slamming into Marc Merit's cruiser. She closed her eyes and propelled herself out to sea with powerful, almost desperate strokes.

In her mind's eye flashed images of Marc—wearing low-riding pajama bottoms, then smiling at a tearful little girl as he calmed her fears, of his hand brushing hers as she handed him medical records or bandages, of his scent, clean and masculine. She sucked in a breath and plunged beneath the surface, kicking hard, striving to blank all thought from her mind as she swam.

She needed this time to regroup, clear her head. Thankfully, tomorrow was Sunday. A day off—unless Sally decided to have her baby. She hoped to spend some time out from under the doctor's watchful eye—maybe reading a book in the shade of a tree, or playing with Kyle. Topping off the day, she relished a rousing evening of chess with Georgie. She even looked forward to ducking the occasional game piece.

She turned toward shore and caught another wave, delighting in the freedom of skinny dipping—the mindless release, the renaissance of mind and body. She felt reborn.

She could hear Foo Foo yapping from the water's edge. As her knees hit sand, she halted her forward momentum with one hand on the bottom while she swept hair from her face with the other. Looking up, she grinned at the mutt. "I said you can't come—"

Her sentence died an abrupt death along with her smile when she realized Foo Foo was not the only living soul poised at the ocean's edge. Luckily, she still had one hand on the sand, so she hadn't risen high enough out of the surf to humiliate herself. Instantly, she hunched in the water until only her head was visible. A wave crashed into her, knocking her forward, but she righted herself, shoving wet hair out of her face.

Forcing a confident facade, she waved. "Oh—good. You're here."

Marc was pretty far away, and the moon was little more than a sliver in the sky, so she wasn't sure of his expression, but his stance didn't look particularly casual. "You're glad, huh?" he called.

She nodded, refusing to relinquish her composed mask. "Yeah. I kept telling Foo Foo to go back, but she won't obey me."

"Sounds like somebody else I know."

She made a face, fairly sure he couldn't see it. "Very cute, doc." Lifting both arms she gestured good-bye. "Take your dog and go away. I want to be alone."

A little too much like Foo Foo in the obedience department, Marc didn't immediately turn to leave. Instead, he stuck his hands in his jeans pockets. "About wanting to be alone, Miss Baptiste," he called, "I'm afraid I have bad news."

She frowned. "You don't mean to tell me you intend to hang around! If you haven't noticed, I'm not dressed!"

He shifted to glance over his shoulder, so she knew he was peering at her towel, piled with clothing. "I noticed," he called.

"Well!" she shouted. "What earthly reason could you have that would excuse your sticking around?"

He ran a hand over his mouth. The gesture was either one of frustration or to hide amusement. She had no idea which.

"I hope you don't think this is funny!" she yelled.

"Not even a little bit."

"*Well* then?" She waved toward the cottage. "Go away!"

"Okay," he said, kneeling to pet Foo Foo. "But I'd feel guilty if I didn't tell you one thing first."

She was miffed beyond words but knew the doctor wasn't a man to do something before he was good and ready. "Well, get it off your chest, doc. I wouldn't want you to be eaten up with guilt." she called. "Tell me and go!"

She watched his slow nod, a good sign. At least he was agreeing to do as she asked. He pulled something from a back pocket. When a beam of light flickered on, she realized it was a flashlight. She shivered, becoming aware that the water was too cold for her to hunker there. "H-hurry," she shouted. "I'm f-freezing!"

He didn't respond, but shot the light up and back toward the tree line. When the light came to rest, Mimi saw something metallic reflecting from one of the branches. "See that?" he called.

"Y-yes. What's your point!" Confused and annoyed, she crossed her arms before her. Another wave crashed over her head. What had been revitalizing a moment ago was now growing uncomfortably cold.

The beam moved to Marc's other side, back the same general distance. This time it lit up a post that stood about seven feet tall. Funny, Mimi had never noticed that pillar from the house. Probably because a pine tree blocked it from sight. At the top of the pole was some kind of box. "See that?" he called.

She was shuddering now. "S-so?" she shouted.

"Smile, Miss Baptiste." The flashlight flicked off and he stood up. "Those are security cameras. Care to guess who they're trained on right now?" A second later he turned away and began to walk toward the cottage. "Have a nice swim."

His revelation took several seconds to penetrate her numbing brain. *Cameras? Trained on? Smile!* When the horrible truth hit, it hit hard. Her mind exploded with the magnitude of her humiliation. How dare he never mention security cameras! She glared at him as he casually strolled away. "You're not going to leave me here, are you?"

He stopped, shifting to glance at her. "I thought that's what you wanted."

Crouching low, she lifted both hands, but a wave caught her and she toppled, and came up sputtering. "The least you can do is toss me the towel!" she cried.

He faced her. "Even if I wadded the thing and threw it to you, it wouldn't make it that far."

She shuddered and drew herself up into the smallest ball she could. "I'm fr-freezing! Can't you walk into the water a little way?"

He ambled back onto the beach. "And get my trousers wet?"

She let out a guttural wail. "Okay, don't! But if you make me walk out of this water n-naked, I'll never speak to you again!"

He crossed his arms before him. "That's a tempting offer, Miss Baptiste." After an irksome pause, he shook his head. Kneeling, he began to untie his shoes. "Don't think I'm doing this out of an urge to converse with you."

"It would never c-cross my mind!" she shouted.

Once he'd removed his shoes and socks, he headed into the surf.

"What about the towel?" she called.

"You'll need that when you reach shore."

"But—but what..."

"Shut up, Miss Baptiste," he muttered. "I'm rescuing you. Take it or leave it."

She shook so badly she was afraid to respond for fear she'd nip off her tongue. So she huddled there, convulsing with the cold, waiting for Marc. As he sloshed in her direction, she had time to chastise herself for yet another half-baked decision. When would she learn to think a thing through, get all the facts, work out the options, before she jumped head-first into something?

He came to a halt a foot from her, and she eyed him warily. "What are y-you going to do?"

"Exactly what I said I'd do." He startled her by shrugging out of his knit shirt. "Slip this on."

She grabbed it, dragging it over her head. Shivering and fumbling and fighting heaving surf, she labored to get her arms into the sleeves. By the time she succeeded, she was breathless and the fabric was soaked.

"Can you stand?" he asked.

She hadn't realized he'd stayed around and almost fell backward when he spoke. "Uh—sure..." She pushed up and immediately collapsed, her head going under. She cursed her limbs for being shaky, numb traitors.

She felt a tug on her wrist and realized Marc was drawing her to the surface. "That was very entertaining," he taunted, sweeping her into his arms. "But your method of getting to shore could take some time."

Coughing and wheezing, she made a grab for his neck. Her mind made note of how warm he felt. *Hot* was a better word. He felt hot and solid and really, really good. So what if she didn't like him, didn't want to be in his arms, not to mention how badly she didn't want to hug him! It was just too bad for her wants and needs that he was like a human heater, and she was frozen solid.

Water sloshed around them as he trudged toward shore. Her body jolted violently as her muscles worked to create heat. Her chattering teeth sounded like a castanets recital. "Th-thank you, doc," she stammered. "That was st-stupid."

He didn't respond, but because her forehead was pressed against his jaw, she could detect the bunch of muscle as he gritted his teeth.

"What is this, some k-kind of police state, with Big Brother watching everything?"

"Just the shoreline," he said. "To detect unauthorized visitors before they scramble ashore to scavenge for gemstones."

"Oh—I see." That made sense. Why hadn't she ever wondered about how they kept their empire secure? It was literally an emerald isle! Worth untold wealth. She cursed herself for yet another subject she hadn't thought through.

He strode out of the ocean, past the pile of clothes.

"What about the t-towel?" she squeaked.

"Could you stand if I stopped for it?"

She gave that a little thought then shook her head. "Not yet."

"You need to get inside."

She had no argument for that bit of wisdom. "How did you find me?" she asked, feeling a little less like an iceberg. The man radiated warmth like he radiated— *No, Mimi! We are not going there*, she cautioned inwardly.

"Foo Foo's yelping."

She spied the mutt taking a zigzag route up the grassy slope and closed her eyes, mortified. "I'm so embarrassed. Do you suppose anybody s-saw me?"

His chuckle was deep and sardonic, vibrating pleasantly through her. "The security division isn't paid to take coffee breaks."

She moaned, mumbling, "They were probably passing around popcorn and laughing themselves silly." She pressed her face into the redolent warmth of his neck. "I may have to kill myself."

"On the other hand, they *are* paid for their discretion," he added. "If you're worried the tape of your romp in the sea will turn up on some Internet site, don't be."

Horrified, she lifted her head to stare at him. "It's on *tape*?"

His troubled expression deepened when he glanced her way. "You don't know much about security systems, I gather."

Now, it wasn't only Marc who was hot. Mimi had gone fiery with shame. "Few jungles have security cameras!" She heaved a mighty groan and ran a hand through her soggy hair. "I'm definitely going to kill myself."

He mounted the cabin's porch. "First, would you get the door?"

Distraught, she shifted, doing as he asked. Once she'd turned the knob, he kneed the door wide and carried her through.

She was startled when he didn't stop, but kept on with his long strides. "Where are we going?"

"To the bath. You need to get warm."

"I'm warm," she said, experiencing a tingle of apprehension. "I hope you don't intend to bathe me!"

He rounded the corner at the rear of the kitchen and swept her down the hallway. Shouldering open the bathroom door, he deposited her in the tub where she stretched the huge shirt out over her knees and huddled in a waterlogged ball.

Straightening, he ran a hand through his

hair, the movement setting off a titillating display of muscle in his chest and arm. "Can you handle it from here?" he asked, sounding slightly raspy. Could anybody blame him for being winded? He'd carried one hundred and twenty pounds of soaked female up a long, steep incline. She wouldn't have been surprised if he'd collapsed on the floor.

She peered up at him and made a decision. Unclasping one hand from about her knees, she curled a finger at him. "Come down here a sec, doc."

His brows dipped. "What's wrong?"

She crooked her finger again. "Please?"

Looking suspicious, he knelt beside the tub. "What now?"

She leaned across the porcelain rim and kissed his jaw. "Thanks," she whispered, retreating quickly. She didn't care if the kiss was another one of her half-baked ideas. After all was said and done, he'd been pretty darned gallant, and she simply couldn't help herself. "I know we don't see eye-to-eye on things, but I appreciate what you did for me tonight."

Mimi had no idea what he'd expected from her, but it clearly wasn't what she did. He knelt there, staring at her, looking charmingly stunned.

*   *   *

Marc laid the squalling newborn in Mimi's arms. As his assistant, he'd had her standing by, holding a towel to wrap about Sally's infant daughter. As he completed his work, he chanced to notice Mimi's face as she cuddled the baby.

His reluctant assistant wore a new expression. One he'd never seen her wear before. A gentle sweetness rested on her features, and her eyes glistened with tears. He sensed that somewhere deep inside his rash gypsy lurked a spark of maternal longing.

She stood there, transfixed, watching the child. The sight so affected Marc he allowed himself to enjoy the show for much too long. Poor Sally wanted her baby. "Miss Baptiste?" he said softly, but got no response.

"Mimi?"

She continued to stare at the child.

Finally, he reached out and touched her shoulder, and she blinked, looking up.

"Give Sally her baby," he murmured.

"What?" she asked in a hushed whisper, as though in a holy place.

He couldn't resist a wry grin. "The baby." He indicated the infant with a nod. "I think Sally wants to hold her."

Mimi stared blankly for a second, and then

blinked several times, as though coming out of a trance. "Oh—sure." She shifted toward the flushed teenage mother lying in the shore cottage's bed. With great care, she placed the whimpering child in the crook of Sally's arm. "Here's your daughter," she said with a smile so loving it made Marc catch his breath. "Do you have a name picked out for her?"

He couldn't force his glance from Mimi's face. Her features were a lovely pink. Her hair, pulled back from her face in a rushed ponytail, made her seem younger than her years. Not much older than Sally.

He'd received Rafe's frantic call at one o'clock that Sunday morning. Marc was awake, unable to put the evening's escapade in the ocean from his thoughts. Unruly visions of Mimi rampaged through his consciousness—of blond hair shimmering in the faint moonlight, of her quivering in his arms, clad only in his soaked shirt. That reluctant rescue had been a difficult quarter-hour for him. The woman had the most outrageous knack for knocking him off balance, making him tense, keeping him awake nights with hot fantasies he shouldn't have.

He wasn't usually grateful for emergency calls in the middle of the night, but when the phone rang, he'd grabbed it as though it were a lifeline pulling him out of a raging inferno.

Now, just over two hours later, a brand-new life had come safely into the world. He took in a breath. Standing up, he smiled at the new mother and her daughter. Appearing both proud and dazed, Rafe perched on the far side of the narrow bed, stroking his wife's damp forehead with work-roughened hands.

Sally looked at her young husband. They shared a moment of nonverbal communication, then Rafe gave a brief nod. Sally's attention returned to Mimi and she smiled. "We decided if the baby was a girl we'd call her after you, ma'am." She kissed the infant's cheek. "Meet little Mimi Doris Constantina Leggett." Her gaze returned to her child. "After you and our mothers. We think Mimi Leggett is a pretty name." She beamed at Mimi and then lifted her glance toward Marc. "If our next baby's a boy, Doctor Marc, we're naming him for you. Marcus Joseph Albert Leggett. Don't you think that's nice?" The young woman's smile was shy and tentative, as though she needed his approval.

He leaned over, gently squeezing Sally's hand. "It's a fine, strong name. I'd be honored." He straightened, acutely aware that he brushed against Mimi's arm. The fact that she moved away didn't escape him, either. With an effort he managed to hold on to his encouraging smile.

After cleaning up and offering last-minute instructions to the new parents, Marc and Mimi headed back to Merit Island. The ocean was black and calm. The night clear. A million stars twinkled overhead. Mimi sat quietly beside him, staring out the opposite window. He wondered what was on her mind. Deciding for some insane reason he needed to know, he turned to face her directly. "How did you like your first delivery?"

She jerked, as though not expecting to be addressed. When she peered his way, he was startled to see tears glistening in her eyes. She sniffed and blinked them back. "It was really something, doc," she said quietly, her usual bravado gone. With a frail smile, she shook her head. "Mimi Leggett," she whispered. "That little girl is going to go through her whole life with my name."

Marc watched as she contemplated that momentous truth, noting her lower lip had begun to tremble. When she bit it, his attention shifted to her eyes. He was stunned by the wealth of emotion he witnessed there. She was really touched. The smart-mouthed gadabout was gone for the moment, and a lovely, vulnerable woman sat there instead. He was struck dumb by this seductive glimpse of Mimi's soft, unguarded side.

Several youngsters were already named after him, but the honor hadn't dimmed for him. He knew exactly how she felt—both privileged and unworthy. He smiled. "Little Mimi Leggett will be quite a woman if she grows up to have half your guts." Though he was surprised he'd spoken the thought aloud, he wasn't sorry. Mimi's cool, collected assistance had been a big help. She deserved a pat on the back.

Her glistening eyes widened at his compliment. For a stirring second, a tear quivered on her lower lashes, then skimmed down her face.

Marc had the craziest urge to lean across the distance between them, run his tongue along her damp cheek and savor its salty moistness.

CHAPTER SEVEN

MIMI hadn't had much sleep, but she didn't plan to hang around the cottage. However, when she saw Marc bent over a filing cabinet, she felt obliged to offer to help. He cast her a quick, narrowed look, muttering he was "catching up on paperwork," and this was her day off. Indicating the door, he turned back to the files, unmistakably ending their conversation.

That was dandy with her. There had been something in Marc's eyes last night—rather, early this morning, on the cruiser—something that had tormented her, making her toss and turn for what had been left of the nighttime. She'd thought she'd seen a kiss in his glance, and for one insubordinate second, she'd responded with excitement, even longing!

Maybe it had been the glow of the instrument panel reflecting in his gaze that had caused the odd illusion. She was fortunate she'd caught herself in time, reminding sternly, *No! You are not going to let the doc get his country-boy hooks into your heart! The man won't even take vacations for fear somebody might need him! He's not right for you, Mimi. Forget about it!*

The last thing she needed to do was close her eyes and pucker up like she had last week in his kitchen, only to discover he'd had no intention of kissing her. She'd been lucky he'd dipped his head to whisper in her ear, or he might have seen her bizarre behavior. She had a bad feeling fate wouldn't give her another break like that, so she needed to keep her wits about her. And she needed to keep her distance from him. The man had a strange way about him that made her go a little batty.

Late that afternoon, Mimi forced thoughts of Marc to a back shelf as she jingled her charm bracelets above little Kyle's face. They both lay on a blanket under a towering pine. The baby gurgled delightedly, batting at the shiny noisemakers. Susan and Jake had wanted to spend the afternoon in Portland visiting Susan's old boss, Ed, in the hospital recuperating from corrective back surgery. Susan didn't believe in nannies, and though there were plenty of household staffers to watch Kyle, Mimi had been quick to volunteer.

She decided she could play with Kyle on the lawn until he fell asleep, then she would pass a pleasant afternoon reading. Of course, Foo Foo had made herself comfortable on the blanket, too, butted up against Mimi's hip. That was okay. She was getting used to the little mutt's unbidden company.

A sea breeze wafted over the three of them like a caress. The day was lovely, tranquil and quiet, except for the tinkle of silver charms and the high-pitched cry of sea birds soaring overhead.

Kyle sputtered and babbled with glee as Mimi jingled her bracelets. She laughed at his uncoordinated antics, enjoying the experience immensely. She'd never spent much time around babies, and getting to know Kyle was proving to be a delight.

"Kylie, did you know there's a brand-new baby girl named Mimi only thirty minutes away by boat?" He sputtered, making a pyramid of bubbles, and flapped his arms. "I thought you'd be excited," she said with a giggle. "One day, maybe you and my namesake can play together." She drew up on one elbow, the better to look down at the infant.

"Maybe you'll even fall in love and get married. Mimi and Kyle Merit." She smiled at the boy. "Naturally, you'll invite me to the wedding. After all, I helped bring your bride into the world."

Kyle made a grab for her bracelets and connected with one, tugging. His mouth was open, so Mimi knew his objective. "Oh, no you don't, kiddo," she admonished. "Your mommy and daddy would be aggravated with me if I let you eat these pointie things." She sat up and separated his pudgy fingers from her jewelry. When he clouded up, she grabbed a rattle and held it against his palm. Quickly, he latched onto it and tried to mouth it, though it was too big. He slobbered on it, then rattled it, babbling with baby enthusiasm. She sat up and crossed her legs tailor-fashion before taking up her book. "Would you like me to read aloud?"

"There you are, Mimi girl!"

That gruff voice had to be Kyle's granddaddy. She shifted around to wave. "Hi, Georgie!" He stalked toward them, his features pinched, but Mimi sensed the ire was totally fraudulent. She grinned as he stomped in their direction. He wore black Bermuda shorts, a red-and-white striped cotton shirt and floppy sandals, looking nothing like the monarch in crimson he'd been the first night they'd met. He clutched a thin, black briefcase in one hand. "What are you planning to do?" she teased, "take a little work to the office? On Sunday?"

He made a grumpy face. "Don't be a smart aleck, young woman! I saw you out here with my grandson. Knowing Kyle is a superior child, and doesn't need much hands-on attention, I deduced your time would be well-spent in an instructive game of chess."

She laughed. "Oh you deduced that, did you?"

He plunked down on the blanket and snapped open the case. Unfolded, it became a chess board with a built-in leather compartment on either side. He opened the partition on his end and began to place white chess pieces on the board. "Well?" he passed her a challenging look. "Don't you want to *attempt* to get even with me for trouncing you on Friday?"

She opened her compartment and started taking out the black. "You did not trounce me, Georgie. You were sweating bullets most of the game. You just got lucky there at the last."

He harrumphed. "Revisionist!" he spat, though she detected a twinkle in his eye. "That's not the way I remember it!"

"Well, that's your problem!" She lifted her chin defiantly, enjoying their repartee. "I haven't played chess in a while, that's all. I just needed a little practice. This time, you're *toast*, buster."

He cleared his throat and frowned at her. "We'll see about that!"

Kyle gurgled and George shifted to look at the baby. Mimi watched the old man's expression soften as he stroked the infant's downy hair. "You're absolutely right, Kyle." He faced Mimi with a smirk. "My brilliant grandson and I agree that your ego needs a good pricking!"

"Oh, yeah?" Indicating the game board, she kidded, "Make your move, loser. I'm itching to show you who *really* knows how to play this game and who doesn't." She patted Kyle on the tummy. "Now you slip off to sleep, honeypie. Innocent little eyes shouldn't witness the carnage I'm going to wreak on your grandpa."

George snorted and moved one of his pawns, but his eyes continued to twinkle. "That'll be the day, young woman!"

Mimi giggled, shaking her head at his bluster. She and her father had enjoyed the same kind of teasing rivalry when they'd played chess all those evenings in their isolated campsites. She hadn't realized how much she missed those contests until crusty old King George came along. This was good. This was exactly the kind of distraction she needed to get her mind off a certain exasperating, disturbing doctor.

With a cagey wink calculated to demoralize her opponent down to the soles of his flip-flops, she made her first move.

Mimi waved a fond goodbye to Kyle, Georgie, Susan and Jake as they went inside the mansion to relax before dinner. Little Foo Foo pranced around Susan's heels, following her Kyle to the mansion.

"You'll join us for dinner, won't you?" Jake called.

She nodded. "Wouldn't miss it!" She pointed at George, making a stern face. "And after dinner you'll give me another chance to beat you. Right, smart guy?"

The older man chortled. "Indubitably! I love a woman who revels in failure."

"We'll see who's reveling in failure tonight!'' She grinned. Mimi had never been competitive, so seeing George's exuberance at beating her was fun. She gave him a run for his money, so his wins weren't easy. For her, chess was for mental stimulation, an opportunity for pleasant companionship, not a need to be victorious.

"Seven o'clock?" Susan called.

Mimi gave a thumbs-up and grinned before she turned away. She knew Marc declined most of their invitations to Sunday dinner. If her luck held, he would remain chained to his desk, knee-deep in paperwork and she could avoid seeing him all evening. She was fairly confident at least some of Marc's paperwork was an excuse to avoid her. That would make it doubly likely that he'd refuse an invitation to dinner, if he knew she would be there.

Why she and the doctor pushed each other's buttons was a mystery to her. One minute they were scrapping, the next they were eyeing each other with—well, something too hot to deny. She could feel the tension arcing between them like a strong, luminous charge of current. Sometimes the feeling was so intense it hurt.

So, why didn't they just fall into each other's arms and get it over with? She'd thought about that a lot this past week and she'd decided each sensed in the other something very rare, something that would be hard to taste briefly then leave alone. Something that, if revealed, would not allow them to go their separate ways without looking back with regret.

She didn't want to be sorry to leave Marc Merit. She wanted to look to the next horizon with pleasure and anticipation. Why burden herself with the baggage of guilt or loss? One day, the right man would come along. As it had been with her mother and father, she would find her soul mate, who would take her hand and travel the world by her side. They would share great adventures, turning their hopes and aspirations into wondrous realities.

That was a dream worth waiting for!

She headed over a rise and the cottage came into view. Without caring to dwell on why, she spun away, deciding to wander around the island for awhile, preferably as far away from Marc and his—his "paper work" as possible.

After roaming aimlessly for heaven knew how long, Mimi found herself in an area she hadn't seen before. A barren area containing a huge open pit about one hundred by three hundred yards had been carved out of the encircling woodland. Curious, she ambled around the site, kicking loose stones and scanning the ground. Stepping near the edge she stared down into the hole, some thirty to fifty feet deep. "So this is the great Merit Emerald Mine, huh?" She placed her hands on her hips. "As far as I'm concerned, it's a big yawn."

"At least we agree on one thing, Miss Baptiste."

She jumped, unable to choose which to do first, faint or have a heart attack. Spinning toward Marc's voice, she slapped a hand over her heart. "You scared the liver out of me, doc! Where are you?"

He stepped from behind a tree and gave her a speculative once-over, then indicated her hand, clasped to her breast. "Speaking as a doctor, that's not your liver, Miss Baptiste."

She made a point to glower for a few liver-beats before she responded. "What were you doing skulking behind that tree?"

He lounged a shoulder against the oak's rough bark. "Watching."

She stared at him, startled. She had expected him to say just about anything but that. "Watching!" She crossed her arms before her. "What—or *who*—exactly were you watching?"

He inclined his head away from her. "That hummingbird."

She peered suspiciously in the direction he indicated, then, to her surprise, she saw it flitting around in a patch of wildflowers. Shifting back to glare at him, she allowed her skepticism to show. "And you were so intent on the hummingbird, you didn't even notice me."

"I noticed you," he said. "But I came out here to..." his brow knit for an instant before he recovered his seeming indifference "...be alone."

She hiked her chin. "Coincidentally, that's why I'm here, too."

He pushed away from the tree. "So you think the mine is a big yawn?"

His change of subject startled her, but she decided it was a good change. They needed to get off the subject of why they were where they were. Her brain had gone to mush. Drat the doc and his mush-making ways. "Uh— well, it's not much to look at," she admitted, wishing she could have coaxed something more pithy and witty from her slushy gray matter.

He took a couple of steps toward her and

she swallowed, trying to maintain her equilibrium. Why did he have to look so good? He was just a man—a man wearing jeans and a beige knit shirt. And hiking boots. Like a trillion other men. And his ebony hair was just hair, the wisp brushing his forehead was simply more of the same-old-same-old. It wasn't spun gold or anything. And those earthy eyes were just eyes. There had to be lots of eyes like his. So what was her problem? She experienced the zing of arcing electricity again and steeled herself against it.

Two feet from her, he stopped and knelt, scooping up a little rock. When he stood, he held it out. "Here's an emerald, or what will be one, once it's been cut and polished."

Instinctively she lifted her hand, and he dropped the pebble on her palm. Shifting her hand this way and that, she could see glistening green within the rock. "Wow," she said softly, then glanced at him. "If the doctor business ever fails, you could work in an emerald mine."

His chuckle was brief and only barely tinged with amusement. "Thanks. I'll keep it in mind."

Rolling the stone between her fingers, she asked, "Can I have it?" She held up her charm bracelets and jangled them. "I collect little mementos of my adventures." She had a thought and frowned. "Unless it's too valuable, that is. I wouldn't want to bankrupt the firm or anything."

He shook his head, his expression wry. "Feel free. I don't think we're on the verge of ruin yet."

She didn't think so either, but she experienced an urge to tease him that was too strong to ignore. "I don't know, doc. With your high living down there in that cottage, I'm worried." She slipped the stone into her shorts pocket. "All that wild excess. The legions of servants. Your wicked, playboy lifestyle." She shook her head in mock dismay. "I'm afraid it's only a matter of time before you're living under a bridge."

He grinned, and the sight nearly knocked her out of her boots. "I should be flogged."

His erotic pull was frightening. Mimi hated the way she responded to something so benign as that brief flash of his teeth. *Benign*! Her mind screamed. *Marc Merit's smile has the power to incinerate clothes*! *Or at least make a woman so hot she'll rip off anything she has on, then obligingly lie down*! *The man is a menace*!

Panicking, she dropped her gaze. Movement caught her attention and she made herself focus on a cricket as it sprang through the grass. "Uh…" she pointed, "…did you know that every human being eats an average of two pounds of bugs a year?" The question was rhetorical. She didn't want to engage the man in conversation. She wanted to babble on about any trivial subject until she could get away. "Eighty percent of the world eats bugs deliberately, but the rest of us eat them, too. They're in every frozen or canned vegetable—"

"What the hell…?"

"People pay big money to eat shrimp and crab." She forged on, taking a step away from him. "They're marine arthropods. I bet you didn't realize terrestrial arthropods are cleaner than marine arthropods. Shrimp and crayfish are bottom scavengers." She took another step away, watching the cricket with all her might. "Insects are low-fat and high in calcium. In lots of countries they're a main source of protein."

"Mimi."

She swallowed hard, battling to ignore him and his dratted sexual pull. She turned toward the cricket, intent on a fast getaway. "In some societies a squirt of ant juice replaces lemon, and in Colombia they snack on roasted ant larvae. You can even eat roly-polies—er—pillbugs—toasted. I've never had the nerve to try one, but I'm told they're sweet and—"

"Damn it, Mimi! Hush!"

She jerked to look at him. "What?" she squeaked, stunned by how close he was. How did he do that when she'd been moving away? Why did his scent make her lose her resolve to keep a safe distance? What was that look in his eyes? Why wasn't she running for her life? "What?" she asked again, this time in a frail whisper.

His expression was troubled; his lips drooped seductively at each corner. She sensed he was fighting a battle, and losing. "Spare me the culinary details," he growled. "I only want one thing from you, right now."

She preferred not to know what he wanted, and she feared if she stuck around she'd find out. Try as she might, she couldn't move, couldn't tug her gaze from his. That steady, earthy stare spoke to her, demanding something she'd grappled valiantly not to relinquish.

"What are you going to give me as a souvenir of your visit?" He stated the question quietly, but his nostrils flared. She innately understood that he loathed his need to make the request, but some wayward impulse inside him forced the issue.

She felt his struggle, for it was her struggle, too. She was stunned by the intensity of her arousal, even knowing he wanted a flighty gypsy in his life as much as he wanted to eat a bug.

She was all too aware of his contradictory emotions, for they gnawed at her, too. They both knew giving in to their physical attraction would gain them nothing except more wanting—yes, they would share a brief moment of pleasure, but what of the price tag?

With every ounce of strength, Mimi vowed she would *not* go off half-cocked! This time she would be fully aware of, and responsible for, her actions. She'd done enough thinking about Marc and—well, Marc—in the past week to know what she dared, and dared not, do. Taking herself staunchly in hand, she pretended his request for a souvenir hardly meant a snap of the fingers to her.

''Okay, doc,'' she managed evenly, flashing her sassiest grin for good measure. ''Here's a token to remember me by.'' She clamped her hands on his shoulders to insure a safe distance between them. Stretching on tiptoe, she aimed for his cheek. If he wanted a kiss, he would get one. A chaste memento, demonstrating once and for all her invulnerability to his charisma.

In the flash of an eye, something went dreadfully wrong with her plan. Though Marc didn't move—not even a millimeter—somehow her lips found his. Just as inexplicably, her hands curled about his neck, her body pressed against him.

Marc made a low, guttural sound in his throat, his arms wrapping around her, strong and possessive. She found herself clinging to him, surrendering to the thrill of his taste and the heady message in his kiss. His provocative intent surged through her veins like wildfire, titillating, exciting. A whimper of need escaped her throat, and she opened her lips, yielding access, reliving the joy of his deep, lusty kiss in the wood.

Suddenly they were on the ground, Mimi's body blanketed by his, his weight, texture, scent, his flavor—all precious sensations, driving her wild. As his kisses trailed from her mouth to her jaw, her ear, he whispered, "Don't leave, Mimi. Stay with me." His questing lips trailed lower, sending waves of delight through her. Sampling the hollow of her throat with his tongue, he whispered, "Stay, dammit!" His kisses, his warm breath, tantalized and tormented. "You won't find anything out there better than what we could have here. Together."

Her breathing was ragged, labored, her lips, her breasts, her womanly core were on fire for him. But his whispered plea—*no, demand*—set a prickle of panic along her spine. *Stay, dammit!* The order echoed through her brain.

Stay, dammit!

What was he saying? Her world tilted ominously on its axis and she felt like she'd been hurled into space. *Stupid woman! What did you expect? Didn't you see it in his eyes? Didn't you know why you feared letting him get too close? Marc is a nester, a homebody. He wants a traditional life, a doting wife and four or five pink-cheeked babies. He isn't an explorer, a seeker. He's a human crutch, taking on everybody's suffering—day or night! You knew the danger from the start. Idiot!*

Angry with herself for her crazy weakness, she shoved at him. "Get off!" she cried. "Get off me and go—go inventory something!"

He rolled away and she scrambled to her feet, swiping at the dust on her shorts and shirt. Stumbling backward, she jabbed an accusing finger at him. "You know what I am—what I want—Marc! You've known from the beginning!" She sucked in an unsteady breath. "I have my life mapped out, and you have yours. Okay, so there's some weird chemical imbalance in me, or you, that attracts us to each other. But don't let that mess with your head. I'm not the hearth-and-home type!" She shoved a trembly hand through her hair, the jangle of her bracelets the only sound. Marc frowned up at her from the ground. As he drew up on one elbow, his jaws clenched. "Don't you dare ask me to stay!" she warned, chagrined that a pleading note had crept into her voice. "What would your answer be if I asked you to go?"

His gaze took on an indignant glint. "Go where?" he asked roughly. "Why? My life is here."

Though his answer was no surprise, she felt its sting. "Exactly," she muttered. Twisting away, she made her escape—narrowly, belatedly and on wobbly legs. But it was an escape, nevertheless.

Marc lolled in the dust for a long time, staring at nothing. When he realized where he was and what he'd done, the sun was making a big deal out of setting. He squinted into the sunset and shook his head, appalled at himself. All day he'd made every effort to avoid Mimi, trying not to think about her. When he'd run out of busy work, he'd ambled around the island restlessly, making sure to go nowhere near the mansion. So, why did fate have to play such a dirty trick on him, bringing her strolling along within touching distance? And why had he spoken to her, letting her know he was there? Mistake number one.

Why had he asked for a souvenir? Mistake number two.

Then...he closed his eyes and gritted out a curse. Then, he'd actually willed her to kiss him. He'd willed it as surely as the sun was setting at this moment. He'd wanted to taste those lush lips again. He'd craved it so badly, that when she'd started to kiss his cheek, smiling that impish smile of hers, he'd thrown out a mental command, compelling her to kiss him on the lips. Not that he believed in such things. But she clearly hadn't intended to do it—not until he'd practically yelled it into her mind.

He stood abruptly. Disgusted, he slapped angrily at the grime covering his jeans and shirt. "Lust in the dust," he muttered. "Hell, Merit, I thought that only happened in cheesy pulp fiction."

He'd never considered himself impulsive, but as Heaven was his witness, he'd *proposed* to the woman! "You're a sick man," he mumbled. "Get a grip. You don't propose to women out of the blue, especially when you *know* how stupid the idea is!"

"Who are you talking to?"

Marc looked up to see Jake strolling arm-in-arm with Susan. They both held clipboards and they both peered at him curiously. "I didn't expect to see you two down here at this hour," he said, trying to regain his composure.

Susan let go of her husband's arm and walked over to Marc, giving him a critical look. "What happened to you?" She picked at his shirtfront and a puff of dust rose into the air. "Have you been rolling in dirt?"

Marc didn't blush often, but he felt his neck go hot. Luckily the sunset gave everything a rosy cast. "I fell," he improvised, unable to maintain eye contact.

"Oh, yeah?" Jake sounded skeptical. "Who'd you fall on?"

Marc eyed his brother with misgiving.

Could they have run into Mimi, who would have to look every bit as dusty as he? Deciding the subject was not one he cared to pursue, he asked, "What are you two doing out here now? It's getting dark."

"Just checking on a few things before we start work in the morning." Jake's expression was too amused for Marc's peace of mind. "We're putting dinner off until eight." He paused, a brow arching meaningfully. "It seems Mimi—er—fell and got herself dirty, too." Jake surveyed his brother with a knowing grin. "Interesting how you're both so clumsy."

Susan gave Marc a close look. She crossed her arms before her, clasping her clipboard to her breast. After a second her lips twitched upward. "Marc, honey, why don't you join us for dinner?"

He swallowed, shifted his weight. "I don't think so." Plunging his hands into his pockets, he thought fast. "I need to go—inventory—something." He winced. If that was the fastest he could think, he was in a bad way.

Jake ambled up and draped an arm about his wife's shoulders. "Inventory, huh?" He nodded, his eyes twinkling with mischief.

"Well, if you hurry, maybe you can 'inventory' her while she's still in the shower."

Marc scowled, unsettled by the vision of Mimi, all blond and soft and beautiful, under the shower's spray. His gut clenched and it was all that he could do to stand upright. "Would you get off it?" he gritted from between clenched teeth. "I'm busy. I fell. Big deal! None of that has anything do with Mim—er—Miss Baptiste!"

Jake's lips persisted in their annoying upward slant. "Yeah. Right." He patted Susan's arm. "Come on, sweetheart. The good doctor is a busy man—and, it seems, tragically uncoordinated."

Susan giggled. "There's a lot of that going around."

Marc pivoted away, mouthing a curse. Lord, he felt like the world's biggest oaf. He deserved to be kidded, even ridiculed! How could he have proposed to the most ridiculously unsuitable woman in the world? Mimi had been right to soundly, even *angrily*, reject him for his stupidity.

Still—no matter how appropriate and sensible her rejection, it hurt like hell.

CHAPTER EIGHT

MIMI sat on the moonlit beach. The bonfire she'd built warmed her; the scent of burning wood revived memories of her childhood. She needed this time outside, alone. Her life was all topsy-turvy lately. Here she was, stuck on an island populated by gazillionaires. How could she have guessed she'd find them so down-to-earth and likable? She couldn't think of a time since her parents' death when she'd felt this comfortable with people. Which was weird. None of the Merit clan were wanderers, angsting to find the end of the rainbow. None of them, with all their money, craved adventure in far-off places, though with the snap of their fingers they could go anywhere in the world they cared to go.

She scratched an itch on her leg, burrowing her bare heels into the damp sand and frowning down at her feet. Then there was Marc, the direct opposite of her kindred spirit, a man so devoid of wanderlust she wanted to scream.

She couldn't fall in love with him! She couldn't let his dizzying kisses and his deep-voiced demand that she stay deter her. She would stagnate if she stayed in one place too long. She would grow to hate him for keeping her from seeking and learning while fighting for the environment.

She needed this time under the stars to get her head on straight. All in all, today had been a frightening experience. She finally faced the fact that she might have been getting herself into trouble, tangled up with this family, while she and Georgie had been laughing and whooping, tossing chess pieces at each other across his plush den. She'd won her first game, barely. When she'd shouted out ''checkmate'' George had slammed the board with both hands, jolting everything. He'd picked up his king and chucked it at her. She'd ducked and grabbed a handful of pieces, tossing them at him. She didn't know when she'd had more fun, even when he'd chased her out of his den, roaring that she was a cheat and a chess hussy. What a hoot.

Luckily, Susan had been passing by, so she scooted Mimi into the nursery where the two women sang a duet medley from *The Lion King* to put Kylie to sleep. It was without a doubt the worst rendition of the Disney classic in world history, since neither were all that familiar with the music. They'd laughed and giggled at their mistakes throughout. Yet, somehow, the sweet, obliging infant managed to be lulled into dreamland anyway.

Rubbing her knuckles across a tickle on her cheek, Mimi sighed at the memory. Drat her, she was getting soft, complacent. She needed to get off this island. She needed to get back to her travels. She'd never been to Iceland. Or Turkey. Or Portugal. There were so many sights she'd never seen, things she'd never experienced.

"Good grief, Mimi!" she muttered, "why did you have to crash into..." She let the sentence die and squeezed her eyes shut, not wanting to think about Marc.

With a weary exhale she lay back on the cool sand. Cupping her head in her hands, she stared up at the starry heavens. A pestering guilt gnawed at her for not getting back to help Marc with the usual Sunday-night hangovers and banged heads. That had been inconsiderate, maybe even derelict, considering she was supposed to be his assistant until he got a real nurse. But, darn it all, he could just deal with one night alone! He'd had some nerve demanding that she...

Quit it, Mimi, she warned inwardly. *Get your mind off that man! Think about the night, the wood smoke, the stars. Anything but that man!*

"What do you think you're doing out here?"

She jumped at Marc's curt question. Twisting around, she came up on one elbow. "Good grief, doc, must you keep leaping out of the shadows at me? You'll give me heart failure!" She tried to locate him in the darkness. Her chin itched, she reached to scratch it, but stilled as Marc stepped within reach of the bonfire's glow. She forgot about her itchy chin, forgot about her need to flee the island—everything but the vision of him coming out of the darkness—became inconsequential.

Firelight loved him, licking his features and torso in a way that enhanced each chiseled line of his face and every muscular curve of his bare chest. He wore jeans, but no shoes. It looked as though he'd been wrenched out of bed on an emergency. "Is something wrong?" She sat up, dusting sand from her hands. "Does somebody need us?"

"No." He halted about five feet from her

and eyed the blazing fire briefly before training his frown on her. "What are you doing?"

She frowned right back at him, but inhaled with relief. At least nobody was bleeding or sick or in pain. Well, except *her*. Why did he have to look so glorious? "I'm minding my own business, doc," she retorted, running the back of her hand across a tingly place on her shoulder. "Lots of people do it. You should try it sometime."

"I'd be happy to, if security didn't keep calling to tell me about your latest escapade."

She closed her eyes and squelched an urge to march up to the offending camera and mouth a very descriptive suggestion. "I'm not signaling a pirate ship, for Pete's sake! I'm just relaxing! Can't your Paranoia Police leave me alone for once?"

He walked toward her, shoving his hands in his pockets. The movement made delicious use of fire-lit muscle. He exhaled, looking weary. "Did you plan to sleep out here?"

She drew up her legs and curled her arms about them. Absently she rubbed at a prickly sensation on her ankle. "I don't know," she muttered, turning to look out to sea. "What if I were?"

"Look, Mimi," he said quietly. "I'm sorry about this afternoon."

For a long time the only sound was the crackle of the fire and the low hiss of the waves.

"I don't know what came over me," he said, at last.

She half turned, then thought better of it. Looking at him, all firelight and taut flesh, wasn't bright. "It's in the past," she mumbled. "I shouldn't have kissed you." She still wondered at herself for that lapse. Unable to keep from doing it, she peered his way. "If you don't mind, I'd rather be alone."

He didn't say anything, so she found herself glancing fully at him. When their eyes met his expression was grim. Slowly his features changed, grew concerned, his eyes widening. He started to speak, then surprised her by kneeling and cupping her chin in his hand.

She jerked away, "What do you think—?"

"Hold still!" He coaxed her face toward the firelight.

"What are you staring at? Have I grown an extra nose or something?" After working with him for a week, she recognized that look. It was his medical doctor scrutiny. "What's the matter?"

"Your face is blotchy." He scanned her arms and legs. "Do you itch?"

She frowned, pulling out of his grasp. Even when he was being *Doctor* Merit, his touch was too stimulating. Scrambling to her feet, she looked down at her arms, then bent over to check her legs. "Oh, no!" She jerked to meet his troubled gaze. "There must have been strawberries in the dessert." She cursed herself for not asking, but it had been so good. "Oh, *fine!*" she cried, scratching her arm. "This is so *typical* of me!" She ran a hand through her hair and felt a welt on her scalp. "I've got some stuff I take, but I'm almost out."

"Don't panic," he said, his expression easing. "Luckily, I'm a doctor and I have stuff, too." He grasped her wrist and tugged her toward the cabin.

As she stumbled along in his wake, she scratched her neck. "Yuck! I hate myself for not paying more attention. I'll swell up for days!" she cried. "After about twenty-four hours, it really gets bad and itches like fire."

"Take it easy, Mimi." He glanced at her. "I thought you were Miss Stoic, who sets her own broken legs and splashes ant juice in her tea. Surely a few welts aren't going to send you over the edge.''

She scowled at him. "Easy for you to say, Doc. You're not the one wearing them!''

He flashed a grin, shaking his head. "You eat insects, but strawberries make you sick.''

"Very funny.'' She clawed at a prickly welt on her arm. "By tomorrow I'll be red and puffy and in agony. That should be a laugh-riot!''

"Oh, hush up.'' He pulled her into the cabin, dragging her toward the bath. "Get under a cool shower and clean off the sand, then I'll doctor you.''

Any other time she wouldn't put up with bullying, but the painful truth was, she detested the lumpy, stinging welts worse than broken bones.

"Okay, doc.'' The itching grew worse by the second. Distracted, she shoved him backwards out of the bathroom. "I should warn you—I tend to get cranky when I'm not feeling well, so I hope you have a miracle up your sleeve.''

His expression grew wry. "Damn. Talk about incentive.''

As she shut the door, her last glimpse of his face revealed a suspicious twitch of his lips.

Ten minutes later Mimi frowned at herself in the bathroom mirror as she combed out her wet hair. Blotchy wasn't the word for what she was. Puffy red splotches covered her face, neck and torso, with more dotting her arms and legs. She itched like crazy and looked like she'd been the victim of a killer-bee attack.

Disgusted with herself, she grabbed a rubber band and pulled her hair into a ponytail to keep it off her back. She tucked the towel securely around her, taking a deep breath for courage. Wearing clothes would be torment, but with the hunky doctor hanging around, she had little choice but to put some on.

She exited the bathroom and came to a startled halt to see Marc lounging against the wall, a syringe in one hand. "Hi," he said, giving her swollen blotchiness his most professional look. "It's worse."

"Oh, not another needle!" Grimacing, she strained to reach around and scratch her shoulder blade. "You've already poked me more than any one man I've ever known." As soon as she said it, she knew it had come out wrong. "I—I mean—"

"No need to explain," he cut in, his expression dark. "If anybody should know what you mean, it's me." He jerked his head toward the kitchen. "I think we'd better do this where the light's good."

He turned away, and she followed on dragging feet. "Goody," she muttered. Okay, so she didn't want anything romantic blossoming between them, but must the fates insist he see her at her bloated, splotchy worst in *good* light?

Clutching her towel, she gingerly perched on one of the kitchen chairs. She wrinkled her nose at the barbed pain in her backside as she settled on the wooden seat. The dratted welts took little care where they erupted, making sitting no picnic.

"This will only hurt for a second," Marc said as he swabbed her arm with antiseptic.

She carefully placed an elbow on the table and lowered her forehead to her hand. "Considering the fact that I'm about to perish in agony, I don't think I'll even notice a needle being jabbed into my body."

His deep chuckle drew her gaze. The brief grin turned into a concentrated frown as he did the deed. She made a face and closed her eyes.

"There," he said, after a minute. "You should start feeling better pretty soon."

She moved the arm he'd punctured to the

table and lolled her head in both hands. "You don't mind if I sit here and die, do you doc?"

"I'm afraid I do." She felt his hand circle her wrist. "We're not through."

She peered at him as he drew her from the chair. "Where are we going?"

"To my examining room."

She hesitated, drawing him to a halt. "Why?"

He turned, his smile humorless. "There's a topical salve that should help."

She stared. "Oh?"

He tugged her along. "Medicine has come a long way, Mimi. If you ventured out of the wild, you'd know that."

She nervously readjusted her towel, following in silence.

"I'll give you a couple of tubes to take with you when you go. And some pills that will work like the shot, but not as quickly."

Once inside the cold, sterile room, he waved toward the exam table. "Hop up."

She experienced a strange muddle of emotions. He was a doctor, doing what doctors do. All very professional. But he'd kissed her this afternoon, and his behavior then had been very—very—well, *wow*, was the only word that came close. "Doctor Wow."

He shifted around from where he was rummaging in a supply shelf. "Did you say something to me?"

She cursed herself and scratched her jaw. "No. Just—*ow*!"

He nodded. After he turned his back she pinched herself for her open-mouthed blunder. *What if he'd heard*? It was obvious by Marc's insistence on using this medical setting that he intended to keep their encounter as businesslike and unemotional as possible. She blessed him for that. She needed aloof professionalism from the man.

After another moment, he walked to the table carrying a tube. Uncapping it, he glanced her way. "Lie back."

She eyed him with dismay. "I can rub it on myself."

He halted in the middle of squeezing some of the greenish gel onto his palm. Glancing at her, he seemed to think about that. "Right." He motioned with the tube. "Roll over. I'll just do your back."

"But—"

"Roll over, Mimi," he interrupted. "I'm not going to attack you. I already apologized for this afternoon. What do you want me to do, write it out for you in blood?"

She saw the spark of aggravation in his eyes and the angry flare of his nostrils. He was quite a spectacular specimen, even when annoyed. He flicked his glance away and then back at her. She could almost hear him mentally counting to ten. He opened his mouth to speak, then frowned, then started to speak again, but closed his lips, seeming to think better of it.

"What?" she coaxed.

He eyed her for a heartbeat, then shook his head. "Just roll. It's late and tomorrow's a work day."

His expression brooked no argument, so she shifted to her stomach. Fidgety, she fluttered her hands along her hips and thighs to make sure her towel hid all the essentials.

"You're going to have to loosen that thing so I can get to your back.

Pushing up on one elbow she looked over her shoulder to give him the wary look.

He eyed the ceiling. "Give me a break. I'm tired."

She clamped her jaws to keep from snapping, "*Oh, Dr. Merit, you're such a flirt.*" Rankled, and puzzled as to why, she heaved a troubled sigh and undid her towel with a yank. "All right, I'm loose."

He cleared his throat, but thankfully didn't make a crack about her badly worded response. Mimi couldn't recall a time when she felt more awkward or uneasy. She squeezed her eyes shut. Her body smarted and prickled, and this wasn't even the worst of it. Tomorrow she'd look like a blotchy beachball on fire.

His fingers lightly grazed the flesh between her shoulder blades, and she jerked.

"Did that hurt?"

She swallowed. "No—you just startled me."

"Mimi, I have to touch you to rub on the ointment. I thought you understood that."

She grimaced and shut her eyes. Of course, she knew he'd touch her, she just didn't know his touch would be quite so—so erotic. In her present painful condition, she didn't see how the word *erotic* could even come up. "I understand," she muttered. "Just do it."

His fingers moved in gentle swirls, first between her shoulder blades, then across and beneath them. Slowly, mesmerizingly, he spread the medication down along her spine. The salve had an anesthetic, cooling effect, and the prickly skin stopped its infernal itching. As a matter of fact, her whole body began to feel—better.

The pressure of his hands was both soothing and surprisingly seductive. He had strong, capable hands. She pictured them in her mind. Tan, steady and clean. He splayed his fingers to span the small of her back, massaging ointment into her skin, quenching one fire, yet sparking another to life. She sighed, feeling quite wonderful. "That's good," she whispered.

One warm hand lifted away, causing her a hitch of concern. Was he stopping? Was this heavenly encounter ending? After a fretful instant, she felt the chill of salve being squeezed onto her back, just above the base of her spine, and she smiled with relief. Her towel rode low on her hips, but somehow that was okay. Somehow, Marc's hands seemed to be exactly where they should be.

As he went back to his gentle ministrations, a tingling sensation began to flow over her. She was no longer embarrassed or distressed, but exhilarated. An explosion of feeling, both elemental and alien, charged through her, and her heart began to pound like a bass drum.

She heard him move, and he shifted his hands, his fingers now directed away from her head. Cool and slick with salve, his fingertips delved beneath her towel, skimming along the rise of her hips. His exploration was potently sensual and shockingly pleasurable. She felt herself flush all over, his bold advance inflaming in her a need as ageless as the sea.

"Marc..." she breathed, needing to say his name, needing to—

"Yeah, okay," he cut in, his voice oddly husky. "That's enough."

Before she could grab his hand and beg him to stay, plead with him to make her feel wildly, joyously alive; before she could even turn and look at him, he'd left the room.

When she'd regained her sanity, she could do no more than stare at the closed door. A lone tear slid from the corner of her eye to the paper sheet that covered the examining table.

Fortunately for Mimi and her strawberry-sensitive body, Monday was a light day in the doctor's office. All the patients were taken care of by five. Marc washed up and began to prepare dinner while Mimi reapplied the salve. When she was finished, she eyed herself in the bathroom mirror.

She looked like she'd suntanned through a holey paper bag. She was covered with irregular red blemishes. Redoing her ponytail, she made a face at herself. Well, at least they weren't *swollen* red blemishes. Only her eyelids were puffy, so she looked like she'd been socked in both eyes. Besides the blotches and the swollen eyes, the salve made her smell like she'd fallen into a vat of varnish-contaminated lemonade.

She'd scared more than one patient today with her horror-movie looks and toxic odor, so it was quite clear she was nobody's idea of Miss America. Once patients were told she suffered from nothing more lethal than a strawberry allergy, they'd quit holding their breaths for fear of catching whatever disfiguring affliction she had.

To alleviate undue abrasion between her tender flesh and fabric, she wore the lightest thing she had, a cotton sundress with thread-thin straps. The simple outfit was light gray, like her eyes. But because of her puffy lids, her eyes could have been orange and nobody would have known.

Deciding she'd had enough of glowering at the strawberry-wrought wreckage she'd become, Mimi determined it was time to do her duty and help with dinner. Sadly, she would rather walk on hot coals than get within touching distance of Marc. Today had been terribly stressful. Every time she'd chanced to see his wonderfully seductive hands, she'd had a melting sensation deep in her belly—a raw longing for things better left alone.

Marc had maintained a strictly professional demeanor all day, so she couldn't tell a thing about his thoughts. But she wondered if last night's massage lingered in his brain with as much troubling persistence as it did in hers.

Resolved to be as detached and business-like as he, she left the bathroom and headed for the kitchen. When she rounded the corner, she halted, startled to see a visitor sitting at the kitchen table. Mimi took in this new addition from the top of her perfectly coifed cinnamon chignon to the tips of her strappy heels.

Mimi noted that this interloper's toenails were painted a fetching aqua that precisely matched her short, gauzy summer dress. Her long, slender legs were crossed in an alluring manner, showing off a great deal of thigh. One arm rested on the table, the other on the back of the chair. Her head was turned toward Marc, who lounged against the counter. His legs were crossed at the ankles. He grinned at the woman, seeming totally engrossed in their conversation.

"Oh..." Mimi said, in place of either a cheery greeting or a snappish "Get out!" For some queer reason, "get out" came more readily to mind. The cheery welcome was harder to come by. "Company?" she finally managed, deciding it was a fair enough substitute.

The woman turned, her sunny expression disappearing and her violet eyes going wide with her first glimpse of Mimi-from-the-black-lagoon.

Long, well-groomed aqua nails fluttered to the vicinity of the stranger's heart. "Oh, dear!" she said, then apparently realizing her reaction could be taken as an insult, she managed a modest smile. "Forgive me," she said, in a husky, not-quite-whisper. "You startled me."

"Enid, this is my temporary assistant, Mimi Baptiste." Marc indicated Mimi with an outstretched hand. "Mimi, this is Enid Black. We worked together at County General in Boston."

"I'm in personnel," Enid said.

"Really?" Mimi bit back an urge to say she didn't doubt it.

Enid lifted a hand, as though she expected Mimi to kiss it. "It's nice to meet you, Mimi," she said with a polite smile. "I understand you're allergic to strawberries."

Mimi walked to the table and took Enid's cool hand, though for some odd reason, the idea didn't appeal to her. "Allergic to strawberries?" she quipped, releasing Enid's fingers and taking a step away. "I thought a rattler bit me—right between the eyes."

The woman laughed, a throaty sound that unsettled Mimi.

"How's the itch?" Marc asked.

She shifted to face him. "Bearable." She had to give him credit, he'd cut her misery to about a third of what she usually suffered. "That's good medicine. How'd you find out about it?"

His mouth twisted in a grin. "I pick things up here and there. Like medical school, for instance."

She felt a little stupid. Well, maybe a *lot* stupid. Obviously the strawberry welts had massed inside her skull and were suffocating her brain. Or maybe the sudden appearance of Enid Black rattled her for some peculiar reason. Trying to keep on track, she nodded. "Right—medical school."

Marc walked to Enid and laid a hand on her shoulder, the nonchalant intimacy sending a stab of envy through Mimi that she had trouble squelching.

"Enid dropped by for a visit on her way home to be in her sister's wedding."

Mimi glanced at Enid. "Really?" *Say, "how nice" Mimi*, she instructed silently. *You should say "how nice" to Marc's guest.* Some wayward part of her took charge, clamping her jaws shut. Why was she behaving like a jealous witch? Marc wasn't her property. She didn't even want him to be.

Enid patted Marc's hand and smiled up at him. "Even though it wasn't exactly on the way, I had to stop in and see how you're settling in to country life." She turned toward Mimi, her manicured hand still holding his. "Marc broke a lot of hearts when he abandoned the big city."

"Really?" she murmured again, fighting a need to ask if Marc had broken Enid's heart, too. If so, from the look of it, Enid hadn't given in to heartbreak quite yet. Mimi sensed the other woman had come dressed to kill. Every detail of her clothes and personal grooming had been achieved with only one objective in mind—as bait to attract and bag

Marc Merit. The signals were so clear Mimi was surprised he couldn't see them. But he probably didn't. This sort of thing registered on an all-female frequency men couldn't distinguish, like the high-pitched sounds humans can't hear but dogs are able to detect.

From the tiniest narrowing of the redhead's eyes, Mimi knew Enid knew Mimi knew. She almost smiled at her mental brain-twister. "So, how long will you be here?" Mimi asked, grateful her voice didn't sound as tense as she felt.

"Just this evening." She glanced at Marc and batted her lashes. Mimi watched Enid squeeze his fingers, then lower her arm to the table. "I hope you're free."

He winked. "As a bird."

Mimi felt a little sick. For the two weeks she'd been there, he'd never had a free evening on a work night. He'd had nursing applicants to interview over the phone and cases to study. Now, suddenly, for pretty aquanailed Enid he was a veritable *pigeon*! She winced at the Freudian double-meaning for the bird she'd chosen. A pigeon—a dupe, fool, sucker.

No, she told herself. *That's crazy. Marc is no fool*! *If he lets himself get caught, it's be-*

cause he wants to. Hasn't he made it clear he came back to Merit Island to practice because he wanted to settle down, get married and have a family? From the look in Enid's eyes, it was clear she had every intention of slipping right into that script.

"I'm thrilled you're free. Now I'm glad I took this chance," Enid was saying, recrossing shapely legs that were, to Mimi's chagrin, utterly free of unsightly strawberry blotches. "Here's my idea. We could go into Portland for dinner, then if I get *really* lucky, you'll give me a lift back to the airport. My flight out isn't until midnight."

Mimi felt like she should excuse herself, but she wasn't about to. Besides, she was hungry. It looked like dinner would be whatever she decided to fix for herself, since Marc was clearly not going to be there.

"I'd better change," he said.

"Don't be silly." She stood. "You're scrumptious." She waved an arm before her curvy body. "Besides, I'm wearing this old thing."

Mimi rolled her eyes. If she didn't miss her guess, that "old thing" wasn't a minute more ancient than yesterday. And if it cost a penny less than two hundred dollars, she'd eat it for dinner.

"Great." Marc's grin made Mimi's toes curl, and it wasn't even directed at her! When he glanced her way, she felt the impact of those earthy eyes and stumbled backward a step. "I'll have my cell phone, so if there's an emergency, let me know." He gave her a long critical inspection. "That swelling around your eyes looks bad. It wouldn't hurt you to go to bed early, for once."

She crossed her arms before her, nodding with mock gravity. "Yes, daddy."

His glance lingered for another couple of ticks of the kitchen clock before he took Enid's arm. "If you're ready?"

She smiled and covered his hand with hers. The move was gratingly possessive. "Absolutely." Her husky murmur dripped with innuendo.

Mimi watched them leave the kitchen. She heard the front door open and close. They were gone, just like that. Feeling like a zombie, she took a seat at the table, opposite from where Enid had been sitting. Without warning, Foo Foo jumped into her lap and she made a pained face. "Ouch, pooch! Watch the claws!"

The little creature curled up and laid its head on Mimi's knee. Frowning down at the mutt, she stroked its fuzzy back. ''I guess it's just you and me for dinner, Foof.''

The dog inhaled, then expelled a long exhale that seemed like a dejected sigh.

''What's the matter with you? He's not going out with another dog,'' she muttered. ''Besides, any man in his right mind would rather go out with an attractive woman who dotes on him rather than stay at home with a grouch who looks and smells like a chemical spill.''

She sat there for a long time, absently stroking Foo Foo's back, telling herself she didn't care what Marc and Enid did until midnight. She tried without success to block mental images of the couple making wild, animal love in some Portland motel room. The shudder of jealousy that rushed through her was way out of proportion to the total disinterest she kept telling herself she felt about the man.

''Foof?'' she ventured at last. The dog opened its eyes so Mimi took that as interest. ''Would I be a bad person if I wished for one of the miners to break an arm tonight?''

The mutt sneezed, then settled back down to sleep.

Allowing a pathetic sigh to escape her lips, she mumbled, "That's what I thought."

There was no spontaneity between them, no spark. At least not on his side. After the long, tiresome dinner, he'd driven her to the airport and muttered her goodbye like a brother. He could tell she was disappointed, but the way the evening had unraveled, for he'd left her with no illusions of false hopes.

CHAPTER NINE

MARC knew he'd been stupid to accept the dinner date with Enid. By the time he'd picked up his car from the mainland garage, he was cursing himself for his uncharacteristically rash behavior. It wasn't the fact that he didn't need to be out until all hours of the morning on a work night that made it a stupid idea. He'd known what Enid wanted, and the notion of a quick romp appealed to him at the moment. After all, he'd been soundly rejected by Mimi when he'd behaved like a love-starved imbecile. She had him stirred up, frustrated and tied in knots, a condition he was unfamiliar with and annoyed about feeling. He'd rationalized that it would be therapeutic to take Enid up on her barely veiled sexual offer.

That had been stupid.

Sitting across from Enid at dinner, he remembered why they'd had no more than a casual date or two before he'd moved away.

There was no chemistry between them. No spark. At least not on his side. After the long, tiresome dinner, he'd driven her to the airport and hugged her goodbye like a brother. He could tell she wasn't happy about the way the evening had turned out, for he'd left her with no illusions or false hopes.

Blast it, why did he have to spend the evening wishing he were sitting at home with a puffy-eyed gadfly? Wondering if she needed another shot for pain, or if she'd felt too drained to fix dinner. Or if her swollen eyelids were obstructing her vision.

Biting off an oath, he let himself into the cabin, surprised to see light spilling from the kitchen. Surely Mimi was in bed. He flicked up his wrist to check his watch. Ten minutes after two. Hadn't he told her to get to sleep early? He shook his head at his foolish turn of mind. "Listen to yourself, Merit," he mumbled under his breath. "When has she meekly obeyed any order you've ever given her?" He was plainly too exhausted to think straight.

Maybe she'd forgotten to turn off the light. He hoped that was it. All he needed was for both of them to fall asleep on top of some poor unsuspecting patient.

When he reached the kitchen, he wasn't particularly shocked to see her. He was a little surprised by where she sat, though. Sporting a huge pink T-shirt, her feet bare, she'd settled on the countertop next to the refrigerator. Her arm was stretched out before her, as though she held a small tidbit. He had to assume she did, since Foo Foo tottered beneath her, on her hind legs, as though performing in a circus dog act.

"What's going on?" he asked.

Both females flicked a quick glance his way, Foo Foo dropping to all fours and barking a greeting. Mimi didn't lower her arm, just peered at him. "Hi," she said, without smiling. "Just getting in?"

He lounged against the doorjamb. "Nope, I've been home for hours. I like lurking in the dining room."

She removed her gaze to Foo Foo and pursed her lips, making kissie sounds. "Come on, Foof. Last one."

"I hope you're not feeding her bugs," he said, forcing his gaze from her pursed lips. Even as tired as he was, he grinned. Why was he so blasted charmed to find a polka-dotted woman with puffy eyes perched on his kitchen countertop in the middle of the night?

She dropped the tidbit and Foo Foo snapped it out of the air.

Mimi clapped her hands and laughed delightedly. "Good girl, Foofer! Now I *hope* you can sleep!" She brushed her hands together and looked at Marc. "Foof's stomach was growling so loudly, she woke me up, so we made eggs."

"We did?" Marc fought a wayward need to take her in his arms.

Mimi jumped lightly to the floor and scratched her back. "Foof's very picky. Wouldn't eat a bite unless I dropped chunks into her mouth from a great height." She indicated the floor, littered with bits of scrambled egg. "It took her some time to learn to catch them in the air."

"Usually Foo Foo eats doggie pellets out of a bowl." Marc stepped into the kitchen, but Mimi held out an arm.

"Don't! Not until I clean up this glop." She retrieved a broom and dustpan from the pantry, then glanced at Marc, her expression pinched. "But, really, eating pellets in a bowl? Where's the adventure in that?"

Her objection was like a slap, bringing everything into focus, and he lost the urge to smile. She was Mimi-the-seeker-of-adventure, the New Horizons Woman. Annoyed with himself and his irritating ability to forget that, he stalked to her and plucked the broom from her fingers. "I'll do it. You get to bed. You look terrible."

She was very near, her hair tousled appealingly around her splotchy face, her swollen eyes mere slits. She smelled strongly of medicated salve. *Damn him*, if he didn't have the most ridiculous desire to make love to her, right there in the middle of a floor sprinkled with scrambled eggs. The mere thought made him doubt he'd ever feel quite the same indifference toward breakfast, again.

Mimi didn't move. Just looked up at him, her expression no longer spunky or cheeky. She looked tired and a little hurt. After a minute, she squatted to put down the dustpan and pick up Foo Foo. When she stood, she gave him a quick, indefinable glance. "Good night, doc," she whispered. "See you in the morning."

"Mim—Miss Baptiste?"

She turned, her somber expression shifting to one of watchful inquiry. "Yes?"

"How do you feel?" That was an inane question; and it only put off her departure by a few seconds. Nevertheless, at the moment, he was her doctor, and that was the most familiar their relationship could ever be. Unfortunately, Marc needed—wanted…

He cleared his throat. "Would you like me to—rather—another salve treatment on your back wouldn't hurt."

Slowly her expression changed; her lips crooked wanly. "Yes, it would, Marc."

Wednesday was an "in-office" day. On Tuesday they'd made the rounds in the cruiser Marc had been using while his boat was being repaired at the Merit Island marina. Mimi's strawberry rash had disappeared and her eyelids were back to normal. Best of all, her captivity was drawing to a close. Marc had interviewed three final candidates this week who'd come to the island. Any minute now he would make a final decision, and next Monday she would sail the repaired catamaran back to its owner and then wing her way to—someplace. She hadn't quite made up her mind where.

But right now, with the waiting room bustling with patients, she didn't have time to worry about that. A summer flu bug had hit the island and was making the rounds among the miners. Sitting behind the desk by the door, Mimi busily entered patient information in files, hardly reacting when the door opened. Without glancing up, she said, "I'll be with you in a minute."

"No hurry," came the familiar female voice. "I thought I'd bring you and Marc a little lunch."

Surprised, Mimi flicked her gaze to see Susan, a picnic basket on one arm. In the time she'd been on the island, she'd grown fond of the freckle-faced woman. "Thanks, Susan," she said with a grin. "I'm starved. In another twenty minutes or so we should have time for a break."

Susan indicated the kitchen. "I'll put this on the table." She paused, her brow knitting briefly. "I—I thought I might stay and eat with you, if that's okay."

Wondering at Susan's hesitancy, Mimi nodded. "Sure. We'd love it. Where's Kyle?"

Susan rested her free hand on the table, leaning forward. "I don't want him exposed to all this flu."

Mimi felt like a dolt and made a self-deprecating face. "Boy, sometimes I wonder why I bother to lug around my head. It does me no good!"

Susan laughed. "Don't be silly. You're just

not a mother yet. That's all." She nodded toward the kitchen. "I'll set the table."

Mimi waved her off with a grin of thanks.

Thirty minutes later, the office was empty and, barring emergencies, would remain so for the next hour. Then the afternoon appointments would begin to pour in. Marc and Mimi washed up and joined Susan at the table. Most days, lunch consisted of whatever they could grab on the run. Susan's picnic lunch was a real treat—thick turkey sandwiches with all the trimmings, fresh fruit of all kinds, except the dreaded strawberry, and tall, icy glasses of tea, decorated with festive sprigs of mint.

Having Susan there as a buffer made the meal easy and the conversation light. Every so often, Susan's expression darkened for the briefest instant, and Mimi sensed something was wrong. Finally, when Marc's sister-in-law cleared her throat and grew serious, Mimi tensed with foreboding.

"Look, Marc…" Susan placed the flats of her hands on the table. "I—I wonder if—I mean I know this is your lunch hour and all, but—I've been feeling a little off lately, and I wondered if you'd mind…." She flushed. "Would you mind taking a look at me? I—I didn't want to worry Jake, so I thought if I could, I mean, if you could reassure me that it's nothing...."

Marc's eyebrows knit with concern. He reached across the table, blanketing Susan's hand with his. "Let's do it, Suze. I don't want you worrying either." He winked, his grin flashing. "Speaking as your brilliant, witty and charming brother-in-law doctor, I'm sure you're fine."

Susan smiled, looking relieved, her blush raging full force. "Thanks," she murmured.

He squeezed her hand, then stood and walked around the table to stand beside her. "Shall we go, Mrs. Merit?" He extended a hand in invitation.

When she accepted it and stood, he draped a brotherly arm about her shoulders and escorted her from the kitchen.

Mimi watched them go, touched by the way Marc was so caring of his sister-in-law. Of course, she'd witnessed his bedside manner for several weeks now. She knew each patient he treated sensed that he truly cared about their welfare. Mimi was continually awed by his ability to calm and reassure people with an encouraging smile and gentle touch.

"Mimi," he called, drawing her from her reverie.

"Yes?" She hopped up from the table.

"I'll need to take a few tests."

"I'll be right there."

An hour later, Mimi sat with Susan in the kitchen. Though there were a few extremely green miners in the waiting room, Mimi couldn't stand to leave Susan to fret alone. She decided the queasy workers didn't need their hands held as they waited to see the doctor, and Marc didn't need her in the examining room with his brawny male patients. Entering information in their charts could wait. She felt it was more important to sit with Susan, unless Marc called her to fetch or carry.

"Don't worry, Susan." Mimi patted the redhead's hand. "You're fine. Just like Marc said." Her reassurance didn't affect Susan the way Marc's had. Though she tried to smile, the attempt was faulty and short-lived. Evidently Mimi didn't have the gift for comforting people the good doctor had. Maybe he'd taken courses on the subject. Whatever, if Mimi were honest with herself, she was just as nervous as Susan.

After what seemed like an eternity, Marc came into the kitchen. "Just a second," he said, shrugging off his white coat and turning away to scrub up at the sink. Mimi watched him with a pounding heart. What was the diagnosis? She glanced at Susan, who watched Marc's back with obvious trepidation. She reached over and squeezed Susan's fingers, whispering, "Whatever it is, it'll be okay."

Susan's eyes swung to Mimi, her gratitude glistening in their blue depths.

Marc took a seat beside Susan. His expression was unreadable as he leaned forward and squeezed her hand. "I don't quite know how to tell you this, Susan," he said quietly. Mimi could only describe his expression as bewildered. She swallowed hard. "This hardly ever happens in cases like yours, with your history of endometriosis but..." he shook his head, a small smile of wonderment lifting his lips "...it seems—you're pregnant."

Mimi didn't know what she'd expected, but it wasn't this. She gasped, her gaze rocketing to Susan. The redhead sat as still as a stone, staring at Marc. Obviously she hadn't expected that either. "I'm what?" she asked in a shocked whisper.

Marc grinned and took both her hands in his. "This rarely happens, but it does happen." Standing, he tugged her from her chair and hugged her. "Congratulate me. I'm going to be an uncle."

Mimi's heart filled with a peculiar, giddy happiness and she jumped to her feet. "Oh—*oh*!"

Susan accepted Marc's well-wishing hug in a stunned trance. When he kissed her cheek, she blinked, seeming to come back to reality. She looked at him, her face flushing beautifully. "It's going to be—a *baby*?"

Marc winked. "That would be my educated guess. Yes."

"When?"

He chuckled. "I'd say around the end of next February. I hope you don't have anything planned," he teased.

Susan's lips began to tremble, and she teared up. "Oh—Marc!" she cried, her voice breaking. "Oh—oh, Marc!" She jumped up on tiptoe and hugged him. "Oh..." She let go, looked distractedly around and spied Mimi. "Oh..." Tears of joy began to spill. With a strangled sob, she grabbed Mimi. "Oh—I'm—I can't believe it!" After a hard, trembling hug, Susan let go of Mimi and hugged herself, her gaze darting back and forth between the two of them. "I'm going to have a *baby*!"

Marc's grin was so stirring, so beautiful and the news so extraordinary, Mimi got caught up in the excitement. She embraced Susan and they both squealed and jumped around in a happy little circle. Foo Foo added to the celebration by barking and running around them in an orbit of her own. Mimi leaped into Marc's arms. "This is wonderful. Thank you! *Thank you!*"

Marc's chuckle was deep and tingled through her. "I didn't do it, but you're welcome."

Mimi smiled. "Yes, you did! You did the tests, made the diagnosis, and gave her the news!" She kissed his jaw. "*You're wonderful!*"

His earthy eyes narrowed speculatively. Though he retained his grin, his gaze was inquiring, dubious. He didn't need to say a word. She knew what he was thinking. *Make up your mind! Am I wonderful or am I the bane of your existence?* She blanched. His stare asked a reasonable question. Which was it to be? Was he the most extraordinary man in the world, or was he a stodgy saint she dare not allow her heart to get tangled around?

A nearby throat-clearing drew her attention.

Susan stood next to the entwined couple, her grin cagey. "I think I'll go tell the expectant daddy that he's expecting—you two go on with what you were doing.'' Before Mimi could absorb what she'd said, Susan was gone.

Without permission, her gaze sought Marc's. She knew her arms still clung to him, but they didn't seem inclined to let him go. Her body took great care to notice every nuance of his touch as he held her. Mimi sensed that his initial reaction had been instinctive, but he hadn't let her go when he'd realized what he was doing, who he was hugging.

They stared at each other for a long moment. She could feel an insidious, slow warmth spreading through her body and it rattled her. But for some bizarre reason, she didn't have the power to break free. Marc exuded a sensuality, a heat, that she couldn't deny, making her want to give in to sweet abandon.

''Mimi,'' he whispered, caressing her with his marvelous eyes.

She shivered imperceptibly at his husky tone. ''Yes?'' she asked, breathless, wanting him, yet fearing what she would find out if she allowed...

''Do you think you could ever settle down?'' he asked softly, his gaze filled with desire.

A fist of apprehension twisted in her belly, sending a confused rush of expectation and dread whirling through her. She knew in her heart that he was going to propose.

She didn't dare listen! Didn't dare give herself the chance to weaken, to take him up on his offer of home and family in a remote little dot on the map—to be a doctor's wife! To take on all his encumbrances and attachments!

With all her strength, she shoved, lurching away. "Don't start that, again, Marc!" she warned, her voice low and tremulous. "It's just like your stick-in-the-mud mentality to believe a person could find fulfillment living a mundane, static life!"

His expression closed. "Many people live complete, full lives, and never travel fifty miles from where they were born." He slipped his hands into his trouser pockets. She sensed the move was defensive, as though he had an urge to draw her back into his arms. She understood the desire all too well and clasped her hands before her.

"Name one," she cried. "On the other hand, I can name a hundred—a thousand—who made names for themselves by exploring! Columbus, Lewis and Clark, Jacques Cousteau! John Glenn!"

His eyes narrowed and his back became ramrod straight. "Oh, so you have to be famous. I didn't realize that." He'd made the accusation softly, yet it rang like gunfire in her ears.

She'd never thought about it, but she imagined that her parents' fame and her need to be a worthwhile person in her own right had affected her decisions. She supposed the dream of gaining celebrity had crept into her life scenario, but it wouldn't help her argument to admit it. "I—I just want to make a difference," she countered, running an unsteady hand through her hair. Why, even backed away from him as she was, did his scent have to torment her, make her weak for his touch, his kisses?

"You think I'm not making a difference?" he asked.

She quickly dropped her gaze to escape the glimmer of hurt in his eyes. Furious with his everlasting logic and for making her feel guilty with nothing more than a quiet question and afflicted glance. "You're twisting my words!" Unable to help herself, she sought his face, his damnable, disturbing eyes.

He looked away; his exhalation held all the undertones of a curse. "Fine," he ground out.

"Whatever you say." With a quick, sharp glance, he indicated the front of the cabin. "We have work to do."

He stalked out, leaving her standing there, trembling and on the verge of tears. Thank heaven she could leave in four days. "Four more days," she mumbled. She had to get away from Merit Island, from Marc and Foof and George and Susan and Jake and Kyle and the yet-to-be-born Merit.

"*Miss Baptiste*!"

Mimi jumped. Marc was furious. Did she blame him? She'd rejected him more than once in the past two and a half weeks. Not many men would be blasé about that.

"Mimi, *I need you*!" he shouted.

Hurrying toward the door, she muttered, "You'll get over it." With all the Enid Blacks in the world, Doctor Marc wouldn't grow old alone. Mimi knew that as surely as she knew the toughest job she'd ever have to do would be getting over him.

CHAPTER TEN

ONE thing Mimi had learned about Marc Merit during these past three weeks was that he didn't take rejection well. For all she knew, hers was the only rejection he'd ever experienced. Everybody got rejected, sooner or later. Marc would learn to deal with hers. He just needed time to accustom himself to it. But she was afraid he wouldn't be all that comfortable with it until some time after she was gone.

That was making these last few days difficult. He glowered at her, barked orders, made eye contact only as a last resort. All in all, Mimi was miserable. It wasn't as though she didn't care for the man, for heaven's sake. He simply wasn't right for her. He had his life mapped out and so did she. How dare he expect her to change all her plans, put aside her dreams for him! How egotistical and self-centered could one man be?

The last time she and Marc looked in on Sally and Rafe and her little namesake, Mimi felt a stupid lump in her throat. She hugged Sally and gave the baby a kiss. In all the years of traveling with her parents, and in the ten years since their deaths, she hadn't had such a hard time facing the thought of leaving a place. Too many people had too quickly gotten a hold on her, notably Marc. The big, handsome sourpuss had done a meticulous job of stealing her heart.

Mimi hoped tonight would be a welcome break. What a great idea, a party in honor of Susan and Jake's upcoming addition to the Merit family tree. Even though Marc-the-Bear would be there, she was determined to have a good time. This would probably be Mimi's last chance to be together with the whole Merit clan before Monday morning, when she would leave and Marc's newly hired nurse would arrive.

All clean and shiny for the party, Mimi rounded the corner into the cottage's kitchen, skidding to a halt when she saw Marc. She'd thought she'd heard him leave some time ago. He squatted beside Foo Foo's dish, petting the dog as it munched on dinner. He looked crisp and casual and painfully sexy in a weathered-red cotton shirt and beige chinos. When he heard her, he glanced up, and her breath caught. That gleaming raven hair, those rich, mocha eyes—well, the erotic combination was enough to melt even a woman of steel. Unfortunately, she was flesh and blood and could only stare as his expression darkened. "Hi," he said, standing to loom over her. "Ready?"

She frowned, confused. Why was he still there, and talking like she was his date? She shored up the cracks in her resolve. "Ready as I'll ever be, doc." She swept her arm down her yellow summer dress for emphasis. "I thought you'd already gone."

"I forgot to feed Foo Foo." He lifted a brow. "I don't know where my mind's been."

She knew, and she didn't care to discuss it. Stuffing her hands in her slash pockets, she barreled by him, her sandals rapping out a hasty escape on the wood planks.

His moccasin loafers, with rubber lug soles, made hardly a sound, but she knew he followed her. She could detect his aftershave; she could almost feel his heat.

"Look, Mimi..." He drew up beside her in time to open the front door.

She paused, peeking at him. "Look at what?"

His smile was crooked and sardonic. "Let's try to get along tonight. It's a party."

"I have no problem with getting along." She faced him fully. "You're the one who's been growling like a—"

"Yeah, okay," he cut in, indicating that she precede him. "Just act like we're friends—for Susan and Jake. They're very happy about the pregnancy. I don't want our—differences to ruin the party."

She tilted her chin, the display more bravado than truth. "I'm in a perfectly delightful mood." She hurried outside, gritting her teeth. Being near Marc was hard. Pretending he didn't affect her in the slightest was practically impossible.

"No you're not." He grasped her hand. "You're as cranky as an old truck."

She glared at his fingers, laced with hers, and yanked, but he wouldn't release her. She aimed her stony glare at his face. "Let go of me!"

His expression grim, he growled, "We're going to act like friends tonight if it kills us."

She jerked on his hold. "Friends don't necessarily hold hands."

"We do."

She scowled at him. "Who says?"

"I say."

She cocked her head, amazed by his gall. "*You*? And just who do you think you are to dictate what kind of friends we are? Don't I get a vote?"

"No."

She skidded to a halt, pleased to see how her sudden stop forced him to swivel to face her. "I'm voting," she said. "And *I* vote we pretend to be friends in the 'I work with you but I don't want to touch you' category of familiarity."

"You don't get a vote, Mimi," he said quietly.

She didn't like his calm. Nervously, she examined his face. "And why not?"

"Because I don't feel like giving you a vote." He turned away, hauling her in his wake.

"What do you mean you don't feel like it?" she demanded.

"Just what I said."

She stumbled after him, his pace too rapid for her to keep up. "That's not fair."

"You told me yourself," he said. "We doctors are gods. We do whatever we want."

She stumbled on a rough patch of lawn and fell. "*Ouch*!" Her knee hit first, and she crumpled to her side. Righting herself on the grass, she checked for damage. A few seconds passed before she realized Marc had let her go. She bent her leg to examine her knee and winced at the pain. Her flesh was scraped; blood beaded up through an abrasion the size of a bottle cap.

Marc growled a low oath, and she realized he'd knelt beside her. "I'm sorry," he muttered. "I'm an ass."

She glanced at him, surprised to discover she wasn't angry. Just unhappy—for both of them. She opened her mouth to agree with his self-assessment, then decided it would be childish and pointless. The less said the better. Pushing up to stand, she flinched at the sting.

"I'll help you."

Marc's arm came around her, but she sidestepped to avoid his touch. "No, thanks." Feeling worn down, she limped toward the mansion. "Let's just get this over."

Marc was disgusted with his shoddy behavior. He cursed himself for the hundredth time since he and Mimi had arrived at the party. Had he lost his mind? He loved her, but she'd made it abundantly clear her feelings bore no resemblance to his. She absolutely didn't want what he wanted. Period. End of discussion. So how did the great, good doctor react? "Like an irrational, macho jerk, that's how," he mumbled under his breath.

"Talking to ourselves, are we?"

Marc started and peered over his shoulder at his brother. "You walk like a cat."

Jake grinned and shrugged. "What are you doing in here all by yourself? The party's outside, on the terrace."

Marc knew escaping to the study was cowardly, and he bit back another curse. Was he now a jerk *and* a coward? He turned his back to the mantel and lounged an elbow on the cool stone. "I'm sorry, Jake." He glanced down at the rich oriental rug at their feet. "It's a great party, I'm just—tired, I guess."

"Then why were you calling yourself a jerk?"

Marc glanced at his brother, for a long minute the only sound was the radio, tuned to a classical music station. He had no idea what the composition was, but decided it sounded too war-like for his current mental state. He shook his head at his brother's question. "Skip it, will you?"

Stalking away from Jake's close inspection, Marc dropped down onto the chocolate-brown leather sofa that faced the fireplace. Slumping back, he closed his eyes. "Look, Jake," he said through a long exhalation. "Go back to the party. I'll be right out. I just..." he exhaled another frustrated breath "...need..." *Mimi*, his mind shouted. *You need Mimi!*

Marc heard his brother's footsteps as he crossed the rug. The leather squeaked when Jake joined him on the sofa. "I gather the romance isn't going well?"

Marc flinched, feeling a splitting headache coming on. "Are you still here?"

"Mimi seems like she's in a good enough mood," Jake went on.

Marc shifted, eyeing his brother with a frown. "Yeah, that was my take on the situation, too."

Jake's expression compassionate, he leaned forward, forearms resting on his knees. "You've told her how you feel?"

Marc couldn't help the cynical chuckle that rumbled in his chest. "She's been informed."

"And?"

Lolling his head back, Marc stared at the ceiling. Around the fringes of his mind he noticed the gilded timber beams. Inserted between them were plasterwork panels with a swirling vine motif. "Good lord, I'd almost forgotten how frothy this house is."

There was silence, except for the symphonic background music. "Ah," Jake finally said, "The infamous change of subject." Marc felt his brother's hand clamp on his shoulder. "Okay, so you don't want to talk about it." Jake squeezed, a wordless show of sympathy. "Come back to the party, man. Brooding only makes it worse." His self-deprecating chuckle was deep and sonorous. "I should know. I was the Sultan of Sulk for too many years before Susan came into my life." Releasing Marc, he added, "But look at me now."

Marc shifted to eye his older brother. After a minute his lips quirked in a wry grin. "You make me sick, Jocko," he kidded. "What did you do to deserve to be so damn happy?"

Jake laughed, and stood. "Got damn lucky." He started to say more, but stopped, his expression going serious. Canting his head, he appeared to be listening to something.

Marc heard it, too. The musical extravaganza had ended and a news program was in progress. "It sounded like he said—" Marc cut himself off. Straightening, he stared in disbelief at the radio.

"...is the only daughter of Senator Lawrence Nordstrom, of California. Olivia Nordstrom, twenty-three, a recent honors graduate of Yale University, nearly lost her life in a skydiving accident today, outside Los Angeles. Her brush with death prompted a quote from the senator, when he stepped outside the capital building in Washington D.C. to speak with reporters."

"My wife and I owe a great debt to Zachary Merit," the senator said, his voice low and gravely. "Mr. Merit risked his life, to save Olivia when her parachute didn't open. I've seen the amateur video taken by another skydiver. My blood ran cold to see this young man dive through the air, at incredible risk, to catch my daughter as she tumbled..." The solemn voice broke. He cleared his throat. "Thankfully, due to Mr. Merit's heroism and skill, both he and Olivia landed safely. You may be assured that my wife and I will thank the young man personally, at—"

"So this is where you two disappeared—"

"Just a second, honey," Jake whispered, holding up a halting hand. "The radio—something about Zach."

Marc glanced toward the doorway. Susan stood there, her smile fading. Mimi had been a step or two behind. Looking puzzled she came to a stop at the door.

As the news commentator went on about the rescue, Marc spoke up. "Maybe CNN has the video." He opened a wall cabinet and turned on a wide-screen TV. A few seconds after tuning in to the news station, a vigorous, impeccably groomed man in his fifties appeared on screen. The caption read "Senator Nordstrom and Mrs. Nordstrom of California."

Looking the part of an indulged matron accustomed to being featured in society columns, an attractive, graying woman of about the senator's age stood beside him, smiling for the cameras and dabbing at her eyes with a lacy handkerchief. When the senator reached the part about the videotape, the screen flashed to film of the rescue, captured by a fellow skydiver.

The footage showed a man, identified as Zachary Merit, as he aborted the spread-eagle skydiving maneuver and plummeted toward earth. Maximizing his velocity, he tore like a bullet, full-tilt away from the airborne camera.

Marc heard a gasp as the man rocketed

downward, and realized Susan had drawn near. "That's your brother?" she whispered in awe.

Marc nodded. "Apparently."

Jake joined them in front of the TV and draped an arm about Susan's shoulders. "Remember when he was eleven, Marc?" he said. "Zach jumped off Doc Fleet's roof?"

"Yeah." Marc nodded, grimacing at the memory. "Convenient, since he broke a leg."

Jake chuckled. "Who would have thought he was practicing to be a hero?"

The film showed Zach's missile-like descent toward the tumbling woman. With lightning reflexes, he grabbed her and clamped her between powerful thighs before pulling his own ripcord. Breathless seconds later they landed, the chute billowing over them.

As the newscaster did a voice-over commentary, the screen went to another shot, this time from a camera at ground level. Zach appeared from beneath the parachute silks, tossing the fabric to one side. The camera zoomed in on his profile as he shucked his harness and helmet. His face was scratched, but otherwise he appeared unhurt. Marc marveled at how much his brother's features had matured since he'd last seen him at seventeen. And he was taller and more muscular. Whatever had been taking up Zach's time over the years, clearly he'd kept physically fit. Still, he was very much the Zach Marc remembered, with that rake-hell grin and unruly mop of black hair. A year older than Marc, Zach had to be thirty-six now. Lord, the years had slipped swiftly by.

The camera showed Zach as he assisted Olivia Nordstrom to her feet. Though she favored one leg, she seemed in pretty good shape, considering everything. Once upright, the brunette threw her arms about Zach's neck, hugging him hard.

"The senator has a pretty daughter," Susan said.

Marc laughed. "Leave it to Zach to rescue a beautiful woman."

"They make a cute couple," Susan added.

"Yeah," Marc said. "Two cute crazies."

"I don't think they're crazy," Mimi said. "They're just living life to the absolute fullest."

"One of them almost lived it to the absolute *end*, today," Marc muttered.

"But she didn't," Mimi threw back. "That's what counts."

"I think Zachary looks like you, Marc," Susan said.

Marc was relieved by the subject change. He knew Mimi's philosophy better than he cared to, and he had no desire to dredge up the old argument. What was the point?

"Now that you mention it," Jake said with a teasing grin. "I think Zach looks more like Marc, too. They're both pretty homely."

"Very charming, Captain Conceit." Susan playfully elbowed her husband. "Actually, I think it's because Zach has a smile like Marc. But he also has dimples, and neither of you two do."

"I can't believe that's your *brother*." Mimi came up beside Marc. "Why didn't you ever mention him?"

The skydiving rescue story ended and the news anchor turned to coverage of recent strife around the world. Marc switched off the set and glanced at Mimi, though highly reluctant to do so. Her scent was troubling enough. "Zachary's our middle brother," he said, working at being unaffected by her big gray eyes, even bigger in her astonishment. "He and King George never got along, so he left home a long time ago. Jake said he showed up at mother's funeral, out of the blue, eight years ago, but he slipped in and out so quickly I didn't even see him that day.'' He tried to shrug off the melancholy, wishing Zach would rejoin the family. Though it wasn't openly stated by the Merit men, they both missed their rogue brother. ''Basically, except for birthday and holiday calls, we don't hear from him much.''

''Except when he's rescuing senator's attractive daughters from sure death?'' Mimi's grin was saucy and impertinent and it annoyed the fire out of him. So why did he burn to hold her? ''Let's face it,'' she added, ''postcards are not nearly as exciting.''

Susan laughed and drew out of her husband's embrace to face them. ''I, for one, hope our daring, dimpled Zachary drops in for a visit one of these days. Even if it's out of a plane. I can't wait to hear what it's like to be the fair-haired boy of Senator Nordstrom—who, I hear, is on the fast track to the presidency, if the buzz is true.''

''Not to mention the senator's slinky daughter's fair-haired hero,'' Mimi added.

''Except black hair isn't usually considered all that fair,'' Marc said.

Susan made a face. ''Thank you, Doctor Funk & Wagnalls Dictionary Guy.'' She took her husband's hand. "Now, honey, if you don't mind, there's a huge cake on the patio that George and Kyle are guarding with their lives. I refuse to eat more than half of it all by myself. My waistline will be swelling soon enough, and I don't need a ton of chocolate-cherry-fudge calories helping it along."

"Okay, sweetheart." Jake accepted her hand. "I hate to burst your bubble, but I sense King George and Kyle may be doing more than guarding." With a grin, he added, "As a matter of fact, I have a bad feeling our son already has icing all over himself."

"Oh, heavens!" Susan shook her head. "When will your father learn to place limits on his grandchildren? He'll spoil them rotten."

Jake's laughter echoed in the den as the couple ambled arm-in-arm out the door. "Susu, my love, I'm afraid spoiling grandchildren has become his major thrust in life."

Marc watched them go, his dismal mood veering to black envy. Listening to his brother and sister-in-law fuss about George spoiling their child—soon to be children—hit him hard. Such a small thing, as world events go, but in the realm of human connections, it was touchingly intimate. Marc was jealous as hell.

"Interesting," Mimi said. "You do have a wanderlust gene in the family, after all."

Marc faced her. She wasn't quite smiling, but watching him with a self-satisfied look. "Yeah, I guess." He moved away from her to save himself the pain of inhaling her scent. Walking to a nearby window, he pretended to look outside, though he saw nothing of the scenery. "You might run into him one day— in Africa or at the South Pole—or on Mars." He glanced her way. "If you do, tell him his family would like to see him."

She continued to watch him, but her expression was no longer a smirk. "Okay," she said, then glanced toward the door, looking like she wanted to go.

He chuckled, the ironic display born out of maddening frustration. "Go on. I'm not holding you hostage."

She flicked her gaze back to him. "Yes you are, Marc. Until Monday."

His gut twisted at the reminder of how anxious she was to get away from Merit Island and all its…inconveniences. Turning his back, he planted his hands on the windowsill. "Hell, Mimi, your boat's repaired and Jake's travel agent can fax you an airline ticket in a matter of minutes. If you're so blasted anxious to go, then go.''

The strains of a melancholy violin sonata were the only sounds for what seemed like a thousand years. Marc leaned heavily on his hands, damning himself for opening his mouth. He didn't want her to leave! He'd rather cut off his right arm than—

"Okay—fine, '' she said quietly.

Her footsteps grew distant and disappeared.

Marc glared out at the glorious day—at the fiery beauty of a setting sun, at elongated shadows falling across acres of exquisite flowers, and an ocean of midnight blue, sprinkled with gold.

A bone-numbing chill rushed through him. His ears roared with the sound of winter wind, the kind that blows grit in your eyes, hair and between your teeth, and screams in your head long after the storm has died.

CHAPTER ELEVEN

Mimi didn't like to think she'd ruined the pregnancy party, but Marc never returned for cake, so that had to have put a damper on Jake and Susan's happiness. Darn her hide! She shouldn't have been so selfish and accepted the invitation, considering her troubles with Marc. Susan and Jake were his family! She should have stayed at the cottage and let the Merit clan have their celebration in private.

Just as Marc had promised, however, Jake arranged for her ticket to Java within the hour. She was definitely leaving tomorrow.

After the gathering broke up, she'd lingered at the mansion playing chess with George until even he was yawning. Eventually, she knew she had to return to the cottage. She had packing to do. It was probably for the best that her flight didn't leave until midday on Sunday. Rather, today, since it was now one-thirty in the morning. She had things to do before she could leave—like returning the catamaran to what's-his-name, for one.

She lugged a load of clean, warm laundry into her bedroom, quietly closing the door after Foo Foo. The cabin had been dark when she returned an hour ago, so she had assumed Marc was asleep. Foo Foo had been curled on Mimi's bed, plainly waiting for her, which had been poignantly sweet. At least *somebody* in that cabin liked her.

The night was crisp and clear, so she decided to throw open her bedroom window to catch the breeze and the scent of the ocean. When she did, she noticed flickering through the trees and caught the fragrance of wood smoke in the air. She squinted and sniffed, trying to tell what was going on. It looked like somebody had built a bonfire....

She glanced at Foo Foo as the doggie did a little turn and settled down in the warm pile of undies. "Oh, *fine,* Foof!" She shook her head at the mutt. "Don't get too comfortable. I'll only be gone a minute, then those things get packed."

She wondered who might be camped on the sand. It couldn't be Jake and Susan. She'd seen them head upstairs around ten o'clock, with Kyle. And she had grave doubts that

George would consider doing anything so bohemian—unless an all-night chess tournament was going on down there.

Curiosity getting the better of her, Mimi headed out the front door and jumped off the porch. Did the miners camp out on the beaches? She doubted it. And it couldn't possible be Doctor Meticulous! He'd have to scrub down the shore first. Yet, even as she poo-pooed Marc's capacity to grasp the emotional boon of sleeping on the sand beside a bonfire, she began to detect the unbelievable truth. The man sitting alone in the firelight, looking out to sea, was indeed Doctor Marc. He'd propped one arm slightly behind him for support, the other was loosely curled around one bent leg. He wore no shirt or shoes. Only a pair of jeans.

His torso glistened in the flicker of the flames; his broad shoulders seemed cast in bronze. His hair fluttered in the breeze and shone a deep, blood-red. She slowed her pace, her heart suddenly hammering in her throat and ears. He was an unearthly sight, too sexy to believe—even with her own eyes.

She noticed the tensing of muscle and sensed he heard her. She opened her mouth but discovered she couldn't speak. She walked on, toward him, mutely and not of her own free will.

He shifted, fire-lit muscle stirring in his supporting arm and shoulder. "Is there an emergency?" he called, sounding tired.

"No." She stepped onto the sand and padded to sit beside him. She didn't know why she was actually joining him, but she couldn't seem to help herself. Hugging her knees, she glanced at his solemn profile. Could she blame him for not looking at her? "What are you doing out here?"

"Minding my own business." He flicked her a dark glance. "Lots of people do it, you should try—"

"—it sometime," she finished for him, her smile self-deprecating. "I know." Slumping forward, she rested her chin on one knee. "I guess security doesn't have a problem with you signaling pirate ships, huh, doc?" She wanted to make him smile. She missed his smile; she'd missed it for days. Unfortunately, her joke fell flat. He merely flashed her a narrowed glance, then looked away.

"Why are you still here?" he asked. "I thought you were anxious to leave."

His churlishness made her tense and upset. "Well, the island isn't about to explode! I had laundry to do. Then there's this ritual called 'packing'—maybe you've heard of it?" She tried not to think about a growing ache in her chest. It felt strangely like mourning. "Besides, my flight's at noon tomorrow. But don't fret, doc. First thing in the morning, I'm going."

He ran a hand through his hair in a distracted motion, then shifted to lean on that arm, too. The change of position displaced hard muscle that coiled and uncoiled with a slow, tantalizing grace. Though Mimi knew his masculine show was unconscious, it impacted on her like a lusty kiss, and her pulse raced.

She was startled when he leaned toward her in an inquiring fashion. "Who's your best friend, Mimi?" he asked, his expression serious. "I'm curious. You've been here three weeks and except for your parents you've never mentioned anyone by name."

She was stunned by the unexpected query and more than a little flustered. "Why—uh..." She shook her head in confusion. Why weren't any names coming to mind? "I—I have lots of friends."

He scanned her face. "Name one."

She lifted her chin, affronted. "Don't be

silly. I have friends all over the world. Tons of friends.''

He shrugged and glanced away. ''Then there's no reason to get defensive.''

She glared at him. ''I'm not de—''

''How did your parents meet?'' he cut in, passing her another questioning look. She wondered what the game of twenty questions was all about. Just a way to pass the time without really talking? Or to annoy her so much she'd go away? She stretched out her legs and leaned on her hands, showing him she had no immediate plans to leave him alone. He asked the question, he could just listen to the answer. ''My mother was vacationing in Egypt with some other teachers, when—''

''Teachers?'' He looked at her. ''She wasn't a wildlife photographer?''

''No.'' Mimi eyed him with suspicion. ''Why?''

He shook his head. ''Just curious.''

She peered at him, frowning, as he stared at the ocean. His jaws clenched, then unclenched. He wasn't as nonchalant as he wanted her to think. ''Did she enjoy teaching?'' he asked, at last.

"She loved it."

"Mmmm." He nodded, then gave her a speculative look she didn't much like.

The method to his madness started sinking in. "Wait a second!" she said. "If you're trying to suggest my mother gave up something she loved to be with my dad—that her dreams had to die for love—you're dead wrong. She had me! She taught *me*."

Mimi drew up on her knees and faced him belligerently. "I didn't turn out badly. I'm better educated than lots of people who had so-called formal educations! Which only goes to show my mother didn't give up a thing!" She felt good about her argument. Totally vindicated, she nodded curtly. "*So there!*"

He hunched forward and brushed his hands together, dusting away the sand. "I see." He stood up. For a long minute, he faced the dark ocean as wave after wave roared in. When he finally turned to go, he paused and glanced down at her. "You've been a great help these last three weeks," he murmured, solemnly. "I appreciate it, and...I hope you find what you're looking for."

Surprising her, he held out a hand. She instinctively placed her palm in his, thinking he was offering her help up, but he merely squeezed her fingers. "Goodbye, Mimi."

Drawing his hand from hers, he walked away.

Marc absently picked at the lunch Susan had sent down for him, but if quizzed, he wouldn't be able to state what he'd been eating. Everything tasted like cardboard these days. His personal life was cardboard, too. Luckily, a steady flow of patients kept him too busy to dwell on it.

In the first couple of months after Mimi had left, he'd made an effort to date. There were several perfectly acceptable women on neighboring islands. Bright, attractive women who would make perfect doctors' wives and give him the family he wanted. A couple of them had made their willingness embarrassingly clear.

By October, he'd faced a pretty disheartening fact. He loved Mimi Baptiste, and until he could exorcise her from his heart, there was no point in wasting the time of women he had no intention of committing to. He knew his decision probably wasn't logical. After all, how could a man exorcise a woman from his heart if he didn't search out another one to replace her? But for some reason, his heart wasn't in the quest right now. So, he decided to give it a little time.

He took another bite of the sandwich, then laid it down. He wasn't hungry. He wished he were. He wished he were hungry or thirsty or excited or interested in anything, anyone, at all! Here it was almost Christmas, and he was about as inclined to deck the halls or jingle bells as he was to perform emergency open-heart surgery with salad tongs.

"Hey, bro."

Marc flicked his glance to see Jake standing in the cottage's kitchen entrance. He lifted an inquisitive brow, unable to even fake a grin. "What?"

Jake walked to the table and turned a chair around to straddle the seat. Resting his forearms on the chair back he eyed his brother. "Susan and I were thinking of going into Portland later, maybe grab a nice dinner, then see a movie. We thought you might want to call somebody and we could double."

Marc appreciated his family's efforts to get him back in the game, but how could he explain to them that he wasn't ready? He had to work through this Mimi-lunacy in his own way and his own time. "Thanks, but I don't think so." He pushed his plate away and lounged back in his chair. "Some other time."

Jake's eyebrows dipped. Marc knew the look. His brother ran a hand along his jaw, clearly not willing to take the initial refusal for his final answer. "Come on, man. An evening in town will do you good."

Marc flashed a quick, hard-fought grin, trying to appear casual. "I have paperwork to catch up on."

Jake's expression grew skeptical. "What happened to the competent and thorough nurse you hired? Can't capable, fastidious Jasper do the paperwork tomorrow?"

Marc managed a brief, well-meant show of teeth to acknowledge his brother's kidding. "Not Jasper. Jarvis. Kevin Jarvis. And he is an excellent nurse. Damned efficient. But this isn't the kind of paperwork he can do."

Jake's exhalation held an edge of exasperation. "Look, brother, mind if I lay it on the line?"

Marc crossed his arms before him. Yes, he minded. Talking about Mimi and how he couldn't leave her in the past and move on wouldn't do any good. His head knew all that. It was his heart that wasn't listening. "I wish you'd leave it alone, Jake," he muttered. "I'm fine."

His brother straightened, gripping the chair back. "But are you happy?"

Marc shrugged. "I'm delirious."

Jake pursed his lips, his expression highly dubious. "I don't want to call you a liar, but you don't look like a happy man."

"I'm fighting it," Marc quipped, his grin forced. "You know what they say about men who are too happy."

"Yeah," Jake said with a frown. "It's a curse, like being too good-looking, too rich and too healthy."

Marc merely smiled benignly at his brother. He knew his rationalizing was simply that, so anything he said would only fuel Jake's argument.

Jake shook his head and stood. "Okay, okay. I give up. Trying to talk sense to you is like trying to mine emeralds in quicksand." He turned the chair to face the table and leaned on it for a minute, watching Marc. "Just for the record," he said, his eyes compassionate. "I speak from experience when I say that pining for a woman is no life. Either go after her or drive her out of your head."

Dropping his asinine grin, Marc muttered,

"How can I go after her? She could be anywhere."

Jake stared at his brother for a long time, his expression sympathetic. The eldest Merit brother knew all about grief. Fortunately for him, he'd finally found a new, bright love and a rebirth of happiness in Susan. After a moment of wordless communication between them, Jake shook his head, his shrug resigned. Moving to Marc's side, he squeezed his shoulder. "I'm sorry, man. I wish like hell I could help."

Marc nodded, "I know." This time his smile, however negligible, was heartfelt.

CHAPTER TWELVE

MARC knew the way to Merit Island so well he could navigate in fog with his mind only half on what he was doing. Tonight was no different, except his thoughts weren't even half on the physical world around him. Heedlessly, he steered toward home after doctoring patients on the rocky isles scattered along Maine's coast.

No longer did he love the mist that hung over the water, nor the tang of sea air nor the cloistered comfort of night. He enjoyed nothing, cared about little other than the welfare of his patients. Apparently that's what a gaping hole in the heart did to a man—left him without the ability to appreciate or even detect beauty in the world.

He'd been such a driven beast lately. Tomorrow was Christmas, so he'd given his nurse, Kevin, the day off. The poor man needed a break from Marc's rampaging perfectionism. If he weren't careful he'd lose a fine R.N. "Damn you, Merit," he growled. "You've lost your center; your temper's shot. Even your patients are starting to look at you funny."

He stared ahead, unseeing, struggling to distance himself from the pain of loving a woman he would never see again. He cursed the endless heaviness in his chest and the damnable loneliness that rode him day and night. He hated living in this shadowland of the half alive, didn't want to believe it was the best he could do.

"*Hell*, Merit," he snarled under his breath, "You're not some weepy widow! She was *never* yours! Deal with it, then move—"

A jolt and a reverberating boom brought Marc out of his mental dressing down. "What the...?" Something had rammed his cruiser amidships, just behind where he sat at the helm. He ran a hand over his eyes. Blast him! He'd been wallowing so completely in his gloom he hadn't noticed the radar's signal. A gut-wrenching stab of déjà vu struck him as he flipped on the cargo lights and jumped off his seat to find out what idiot had run into him.

Moving to the side where he'd been hit, he squinted into the fog, now brightly lit. It wasn't hard to distinguish the front of a small catamaran. The bows of both hulls were crumpled against his cruiser. The fiberglass on the side of his boat was damaged and the gelcoat marred.

He bit back a curse. Did somebody paint a bull's-eye on the side of his cruiser? What was it with fog and catamarans and his boat?

Out of the corner of his eye, Marc saw somebody slowly rise to stand, hooking an arm around the mast to steady herself on the canvas trampoline. His frown deepened. Why did the petite, one-man strike force look so painfully like Mimi? Even in the long pants and jacket, she seemed so—so familiar. He winced, rubbing his eyes with the heels of his hands. He hadn't gotten much sleep lately, but he didn't think he was so far gone that he'd start hallucinating.

The woman let out a wail and ran a hand through a blond mass of hair. "Oh, no!" Her gaze lifted to fix on Marc and she jabbed a finger at the damage to her prow. "Look what you did to my boat!"

Marc stared at her in disbelief. She sounded like Mimi, too!

"Well," she called, after a minute. "Don't you have anything to say?" Fisting her hands on her hips, she eyed him. "Like, maybe,

'How thoughtless of you to ram the side of your boat into the front of mine'?''

He leaned on the gunwale, staring at her. "Mimi?" Her name was a whisper of doubt.

"Then I say, 'But this isn't even my boat!'" She started making her way carefully toward him.

"Lord...!"

"No, that's not next, doc. You're supposed to say, real sarcastic like, 'I suppose you were just passing by when you heard the crash and decided to investigate?'" She scurried along the damaged hull nearest him. When she reached the side of his boat, she rested her hands between his and looked up at him. Soft, smoke-gray eyes were round and watchful. Her fine hair drifted artlessly about her shoulders in a sudden breeze and her sweet scent wafted up, bringing back memories both wonderful and terrible. "What are you doing?" he whispered.

She smiled faintly and shook her head. "No, you're supposed to tell me I've hit my head and you have to doctor it, then you invite me aboard."

He was confused, but something inside him began to glow. He didn't quite feel like grinning, yet. She could merely be passing through on another adventure. "Your head's not bleeding, Mimi," he said, trying to sound reasonable, but it came out more guarded.

She reached up and felt around her scalp, then gave him a shrug. "Seems I learn from my mistakes." She smiled then, and his heart clenched. Did he dare hope this was more than a brief interlude in her quest for adventure?

She lifted a hand as though asking for him to take it. "But I've damaged your boat and I can't sail mine the way it is. I guess I'm going to have to work it off again, doc."

Without engaging his brain in the matter, he lifted her aboard. She landed a bit unsteadily, swaying into him. Hugging his waist she looked up. "Oops. Clumsy me." He didn't know what to do, so he just stared at her. After a second, she righted herself and took a step away. "What about it?"

"What about what?" Maybe he'd hit *his* head, this time.

She looked away and took a deep breath before facing him again. "What about me working for you until I pay for the damage?"

He ran a hand through his hair, feeling off-center. "I have a nurse, Mimi."

She shrugged and peered at him, her brows

slightly knit. "So, how do you suggest I pay, doc?"

He noticed a chain glistening around her neck. The jacket was open enough for him to see the rough emerald he'd given her, dangling from it. Hooking his finger around the chain, he lifted it. "That would pay for it."

Without lowering her gaze, she shook her head. "Sorry, I can't part with that. It reminds me of a man I once knew."

Puzzled by the way she said it, he heard himself ask, "Somebody you liked?"

"No." She smiled in her sassy way, and his heart dropped to his feet. "Somebody I love."

The statement stunned Marc into speechlessness. A feeling of disorientation flooded him. He could only stare, flummoxed.

In the silence, Mimi swallowed, then a determined look passed over her features and she seemed to decide to forge on. "He's a stick-in-the-mud doctor, and I'm an explorer, so naturally it couldn't work out."

He watched her, frowning. What *was* this game—"Drive Marc Merit Nuts for Sport"?

"Don't you have *anything* to say?" she asked.

He watched her warily. She had such devastating power over his heart, he didn't want to risk more damage. "Like what?" he asked, his tone skeptical.

"Like you want me to stay, you idiot!" she cried, grasping his hands. "Like you've been miserable without me, and you *love* me, you fool!"

He stared, feeling everything go silent inside him. He'd spent so many days and nights tossing and turning in bleak desolation. Did he dare believe his suffering might be coming to an end? Did he dare risk opening himself up to the possibility of more hurt?

Good Lord, man, yes! he told himself. *Do you want to go on being an emotional android? Do you want Mimi or don't you? She's here, dammit! Say something now—even if she's playing some kind of bored gypsy's game—or you'll regret it for the rest of your life!*

"All right," he said, solemnly. "I want you to stay, Mimi; I've been miserable without you and I love you—more than life."

Now it was her turn to stare. Wide-eyed, she squeaked, "You—you *do*?"

He could see sweet vulnerability glisten in her eyes, and her lower lip began to tremble. Suddenly he knew all that flippancy she exhibited had been a front. She wasn't nearly as sassy and sure of herself as she wanted him to believe. The sight of her tears, shimmering in her eyes and glistening on her lower lashes, filled him with happiness so overpowering it physically jolted him, like an electrical shock. He'd never realized such a pure, rich emotion was possible. At long, long last, he was able to smile again. "Of course, I do—you little idiot."

She sniffed, running the back of her hand along her cheek to wipe away a tear. "Well, what are you going to do about it?"

He felt a stitch in his heart. "What can I do, if you're just passing through, wrecking boats?" he asked, surprised that even now he still wasn't quite willing to lay aside his defenses.

"What if I weren't just passing through?" she asked, a tremor in her voice. She blinked, and tears fell, skimming along her cheeks. "What would you say?"

Reaching up on tiptoe, she grazed his lips with hers, whispering, "I was so selfish and self-centered I couldn't see the truth when it was right there before my eyes. After I left you, I realized traveling the world wasn't the part of my life that had been meaningful to me. It had been belonging to a loving family—there for each other no matter where in the world we found ourselves.''

She kissed the corner of his mouth so softly Marc was mesmerized, unable to move for fear this dream would evaporate as quickly and as strangely as it had appeared. ''While I was here with you and your family,'' she said, ''I glimpsed that possibility of closeness again, but I wouldn't let myself see it—until...'' Her voice broke and she swallowed, backing slightly away. Her smile was tremulous and dear as she searched his face, seeming to find something charming in his expression.

''Besides, I want to teach you about roasting chestnuts over an open fire.'' Tender promises filled her eyes and honeyed her voice. ''There's this game that's fun to play, where you give a name to each chestnut sitting, roasting, in a row. The first nut to pop is the true love who will ask you to marry him.'' She smoothed a stray lock of hair off his forehead, tilting her chin up to tease his lips with hers. ''Since nobody's asked me—lately—it should be enlightening.'' She kissed him softly. ''Don't you agree?''

The brush of her lips sent a wave of desire raging through his body, its intensity unnerving. Marc was suddenly very much the man in control that he'd been six months ago, before Mimi had heisted his heart. A grin came to life on his lips. "I don't think so, Mimi," he countered.

She drew away, blinking, her expression suddenly cautious, all teasing gone. "No?" She swallowed several times, and Marc could see he'd rattled her.

Feeling like a fool he took her into his arms, hugging her to him. "Oh, darling, I meant— we'll play the game to name our first child, because..." he lowered his lips to hers, drinking deeply of the taste he'd dreamed of for so long and despaired of ever savoring again. "...because—Mimi..." he murmured, teasing her mouth with his, "I want you to be my wife." His kiss was brief, but made erotic promises he intended to keep. "Will you marry me?"

With her arms curled about his neck, she pressed her delicious body into his, lolling her head back to smile into his eyes. "I wouldn't want to go into any marriage owing a debt," she teased. Her fingers massaged his nape, driving him wild. "How do you want me to pay for the damage to your boat?"

His chuckle came from a deep, hidden place, a place he hadn't believed could experience such joy. Drawing her down on a cushioned bench, he warned with a grin, "That had better be a yes."

"Yes—oh, yes, Marc. It's so good to be home," she murmured through a sigh, taking his face in her hands. "Darling, loving you will be one beautiful discovery after another. Anything I could have done out there, alone, will be greater, more rewarding shared with you, on Merit Island—or anywhere else—just so long as we're together."

The truth in her eyes thrilled him to his core and his gut heated with a wild, new passion that he knew would never be quenched. Taking the woman he loved into the haven of his body, Marc felt secure, deep in his soul. Mimi had finally found her home—and he, his heart.

* * * * *

Read how bad-boy Zach Merit
tangles with prim and proper
Olivia Nordstrom
as fate pushes them together
to hide out on Merit Island.

Zach Merit's story.
Coming soon from Renee Roszel

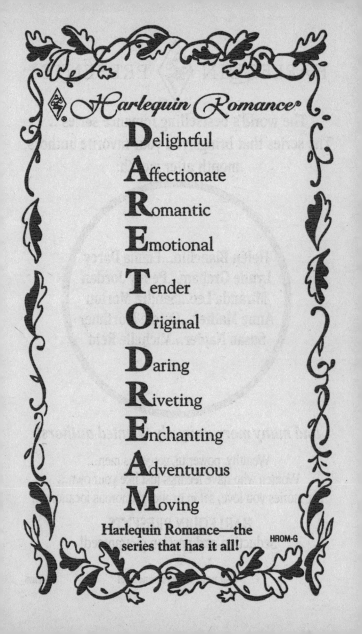

Harlequin Romance®

Delightful

Affectionate

Romantic

Emotional

Tender

Original

Daring

Riveting

Enchanting

Adventurous

Moving

Harlequin Romance—the
series that has it all!

HROM-G

HARLEQUIN ◆ PRESENTS®

The world's bestselling romance series...
The series that brings you your favorite authors,
month after month:

Helen Bianchin...Emma Darcy
Lynne Graham...Penny Jordan
Miranda Lee...Sandra Morton
Anne Mather...Carole Mortimer
Susan Napier...Michelle Reid

and many more uniquely talented authors!

Wealthy, powerful, gorgeous men...
Women who have feelings just like your own...
The stories you love, set in exotic, glamorous locations...

HARLEQUIN PRESENTS,
Seduction and passion guaranteed!

Visit us at www.romance.net

Harlequin® Historical

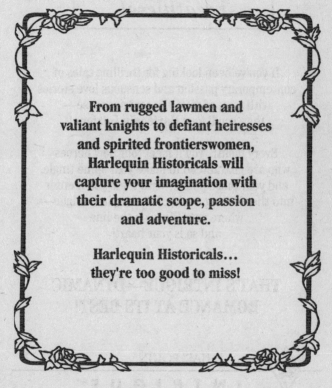

From rugged lawmen and
valiant knights to defiant heiresses
and spirited frontierswomen,
Harlequin Historicals will
capture your imagination with
their dramatic scope, passion
and adventure.

Harlequin Historicals…
they're too good to miss!

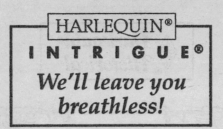